THE BLOOD OF RENEGADES

Center Point
Large Print

Also by J. A. Johnstone and available from
Center Point Large Print:

Big Gundown
Seven Days to Die
Rattlesnake Valley
Bounty Killers
Trail of Blood

Also by William W. Johnstone and
J. A. Johnstone:

Mankiller, Colorado
Deadwood Gulch
Helltown Massacre
Violent Land
Hard Ride to Hell
Butcher of Bear Creek

**This Large Print Book carries the
Seal of Approval of N.A.V.H.**

The Loner:

THE BLOOD OF RENEGADES

J. A. JOHNSTONE

CENTER POINT LARGE PRINT
THORNDIKE, MAINE

This Center Point Large Print edition is published
in the year 2014 by arrangement with
Kensington Publishing Corp.

The text of this Large Print edition is unabridged.
In other aspects, this book may vary
from the original edition.
Printed in the United States of America
on permanent paper.
Set in 16-point Times New Roman type.

ISBN: 978-1-62899-053-9

Library of Congress Cataloging-in-Publication Data

Johnstone, J. A.
The blood of renegades : the loner / J.A. Johnstone. —
    Center Point Large Print edition.
    pages cm
    ISBN 978-1-62899-053-9 (Library binding : alk. paper)
    1. Texas—Fiction. 2. Large type books. I. Title.
    PS3610.O43B56 2014
    813′.6—dc23
                                                    2013050327

THE BLOOD OF
RENEGADES

Chapter 1

Rugged, snow-capped mountains rose in the distance, a majestic sight under a beautiful blue sky.

The same couldn't be said about the terrain over which Conrad Browning and Arturo Vincenzo traveled. There was nothing majestic about it. The landscape was mostly flat and semiarid, sparsely covered by tough grass, dotted with scrubby mesquites and greasewood, and slashed by the occasional arroyo.

Hardly the oasis Brigham Young had promised his followers, Conrad mused, but the Mormons had made their homes in Utah anyway and in most cases seemed to be thriving, if bustling Salt Lake City was any indication. Conrad and Arturo had passed through the city a few days earlier and since then had been making their way around the huge salt lake that gave the place its name. Following the railroad that skirted the northern end of the lake they had left the vast body of water behind them and angled south-westward toward Nevada.

Conrad rode a big, blaze-faced black gelding while Arturo handled the reins hitched to the four-horse team pulling the buggy. They had been together for several months after leaving Boston and embarking on a cross-country quest for Conrad's lost children, little Frank and Vivian. The children's mother, the vengeful Pamela Tarleton, had concealed their very existence from Conrad, who hadn't known she was pregnant when he broke their engagement and married Rebel Callahan instead.

A lot of time and tragedy had gone by since then. Rebel and Pamela were dead, but Pamela had managed to strike at Conrad from beyond the grave. Her cousin had delivered the letter she had written revealing Conrad had a son and daughter—twins, Pamela boasted—who were hidden where he would never find them.

It was a particularly vicious way of tormenting him, but he wasn't the sort to suffer without trying to do something about it. His investigation had uncovered the fact that Pamela had taken the twins from Boston and started to San Francisco with them. Since then, Conrad and his friend and servant Arturo had been searching for them, following Pamela's route across the country. Conrad had no way of knowing whether she had taken the children with her all the way to the coast, so he and Arturo stopped frequently along the way to ask questions and find out if anybody knew anything about a woman traveling with a nanny and two small children.

But there wasn't anybody to ask questions of,

out there in the thinly-populated wilderness. Often the steel rails of the Southern Pacific and the telegraph poles and wires erected by Western Union were the only signs civilization had ever visited the area. No more settlements of any size lay between there and Nevada, at least none Conrad knew of.

He was a tall, well-built man in his twenties with close-cropped sandy hair under his flat-crowned black Stetson. Once he had been so handsome he'd set the hearts of society girls all over Boston—and the hearts of their mothers—to fluttering, but time and trouble had etched character lines in his face. He wore a white shirt and black boots, trousers, and coat. A hand-tooled black gunbelt was strapped around his trim hips. A meticulously cared for Colt revolver with walnut grips rode in the holster attached to the gunbelt.

In addition to the handgun, Conrad carried a Winchester repeater and a heavy-caliber Sharps carbine in sheaths lashed to his saddle. He was an expert with all three weapons but perhaps most deadly with the Colt, which was fitting since he was the son of Frank Morgan—one of the fastest men to ever strap on a six-gun. Morgan was known as The Drifter, and some called him the last true gunfighter.

That might have been true once, but no more. Now there was the man who called himself Kid Morgan, and while Conrad didn't go out of his way to keep it a secret, not all that many people knew Kid Morgan and Conrad Browning were one and the same. He had invented the identity to help him track down Rebel's killers, and it still came in handy from time to time.

More than a month earlier, while they were in Denver searching for clues to where Pamela might have taken the children, Conrad and Arturo had gotten roped into some trouble that left Arturo with a wounded arm. Since then, they'd been traveling at a slower pace so his injury would have more time to heal. Conrad had handled the buggy for a while, but Arturo's arm was stronger and he had resumed his driving chores. That was fine with Conrad. He preferred being in the saddle.

"My word, there's really not much out here, is there?" Arturo said. "I thought Wyoming was godforsaken, but this is just depressing."

Conrad smiled. "I don't know. It has a certain stark beauty about it, don't you think?"

"For about the first ten minutes. After that it's just flat and empty and ugly."

Conrad couldn't argue with that. It seemed like a pretty accurate assessment to him. Still ahead of them in Nevada were areas like that, but eventually they would get into the prettier country around Reno and Carson City.

Carson City . . . Just thinking about the place threatened to send waves of melancholy sweeping over Conrad's soul. It was where he and Rebel had lived when she was murdered. Their home had gone up in flames, and for a while everyone believed Conrad had perished in the blaze.

He'd wanted them to think that. Kid Morgan was born then and he'd set out on his mission of vengeance.

Unexpectedly, vengeance had turned out to not be very satisfying. Conrad had drifted for a while after, but violence and death seemed to dog his trail. The revelation about the twins had changed everything.

Arturo broke in on Conrad's thoughts. "How long will it take for us to get to those mountains?"

Conrad studied the snow-mantled peaks. "Maybe late today, maybe early tomorrow. We'll have to follow the railroad through the passes. There may be other ways through, but I don't know them."

"We could be in San Francisco tomorrow if we took the train."

"Yes, we could, but what if Pamela hid the twins somewhere along the way?"

"I'm familiar with that logic," Arturo said. "I wasn't suggesting that we *should* take the train, but rather just commenting on the relative speed with which it could deliver us to our destination. Isn't it amazing?"

"Yeah," Conrad said. "Amazing." As he spoke he was distracted by a cloud of dust he spotted north of the railroad tracks. Squinting toward the dust he watched it drift closer.

Arturo noticed where Conrad was looking, and turned his head, studying the desert country in that direction, too. "Someone's coming."

"Yeah," Conrad said. "Fast, too."

And that usually meant trouble.

Conrad reined in his horse and Arturo brought the buggy to a stop. As they watched, the dust column continued to move toward them. Conrad's keen eyes made out a single figure at the base of the column. His gaze shifted and he lifted a hand to point. "Even more dust back there."

"What does it mean?" Arturo asked.

"Means that fella in front is being chased by at least half a dozen riders, and I'll bet they don't have anything good in mind for him."

Arturo's eyes narrowed suspiciously as he looked at Conrad. "What exactly are we going to do about it?"

With a faint smile, Conrad said, "Now that's a good question."

He reached for his Winchester and drew it out of the saddle boot.

"I knew it!" Arturo said. "Whatever this trouble is, you're going to get mixed up right in the middle of it, aren't you? You can't let it gallop on past us."

Conrad didn't answer with words. He heeled his horse into a run across the arid plains in a course that would intercept the fleeing rider.

Chapter 2

Behind him, Arturo yelled something but Conrad couldn't make it out over the thunder of the black's hoofbeats. He leaned forward in the saddle and urged the animal to greater speed.

He had been torn for only a second between the two courses of action that lay before him. He and Arturo could stay where they were and allow the pursuit to pass in front of them and continue on to the south, which was probably the smartest thing to do, since he was on an important mission of his own: finding his lost children.

Or he could give in to the part of him that didn't like six-to-one odds.

That was the urge that won the mental battle. He had gotten in the habit of sticking up for anybody who was outnumbered.

It was possible the fleeing rider was a killer or a train robber or some other sort of outlaw with a posse on his trail. In that case Conrad could stop the fugitive and do a favor for the law. But he had to get an idea of what was going on. He didn't hear any shots or see any puffs of powdersmoke from the pursuers. Evidently they weren't out to kill the person they were after.

Suddenly, Conrad realized he needed to stop

thinking of that lone rider as a man. He was close enough to see long, fair hair streaming out behind the rider's head. Some men wore their hair long like that, but Conrad's instincts told him the single rider was a woman.

A woman being chased by that many men was bound to be in trouble. Hauling back on the reins he brought his mount to a stop. He levered a round into the Winchester's firing chamber and brought the rifle to his shoulder. Aiming high, he squeezed the trigger and sent a shot blasting over the heads of the pursuers, who were a couple hundred yards away.

The woman was closer, maybe fifty yards from him. She changed course, veering toward him, hoping he would protect her. Conrad levered the rifle and squeezed off another round.

The pursuers didn't return his fire. As the woman flashed past Conrad without slowing down he caught a glimpse of her pale, frightened face. Glancing over his shoulder after her, he saw Arturo had followed him in the buggy and was stopped a short distance away. He had jumped down from the vehicle and stood with a rifle in his hands, ready to get into the fight if need be.

Conrad turned his attention back to the pursuers, who slowed their horses and then stopped, evidently unwilling to charge right into the threat of two Winchesters. They were far enough away Conrad couldn't make out any details about them except the broad-brimmed hats and long dusters they wore. The horses milled around as the dust cloud kicked up by their hooves started to blow away.

Seconds passed in nerve-stretching tension. Finally one of the men prodded his horse forward. Conrad stayed where he was, waiting in motionless silence, as the man rode slowly toward him.

"That's far enough," Conrad called when the man was about thirty feet away.

"Mister, I don't know who you are, but you're mixin' in somethin' that's none of your concern." The spokesman for the pursuers was a thick-set man with dark beard stubble on his face. One eye was squeezed almost shut, no doubt from the injury that had left a scar angling away from it. "That woman belongs to us."

Conrad said, "You may not have heard, but it's almost a new century. Enlightened people are starting to believe women don't actually belong to anyone except themselves."

The man grunted. "It don't matter what century it is. The law's the law."

"What law?"

"The law of God!" the man thundered.

With that, things became clearer to Conrad. "You're Mormons, aren't you?"

"Call ourselves saints," the man said. "Or in our case . . . angels."

Avenging angels, Conrad thought. Gun-packing enforcers for the leaders of the Mormon hierarchy. Conrad had heard stories about them, but these were the first he had encountered. When he'd been in charge of all the Browning business and financial interests—back in that other life of his before everything he held dear was ripped away from him—he had dealt at times with Mormon leaders. You couldn't do business in Utah without dealing with the Mormons. But they had been businessmen as much as they were church elders, their religious beliefs tempered by the desire to make money. These gunmen were very different sorts.

Despite being outnumbered, Conrad wasn't afraid of them. "Chasing a scared girl across this wasteland doesn't strike me as being very religious."

The man scowled and jabbed a finger at him, as if to strike him dead. "Don't you presume to know the will of the Lord! The girl is ours and she goes back with us. She has defied the elders and must be punished!"

"You'll have to take her from us," Conrad said coolly.

"There are six of us and two of you," the man pointed out with a sneer.

"Yes, but we'll kill four of you before you put us down. Maybe five. Maybe even all six." Conrad smiled. "Not to brag, but I'm pretty good

16

with a gun. Maybe we'll all wind up lying here, food for the buzzards, and then the girl will ride away. What good will that do your elders?"

The other men had been listening intently to the exchange. One of them spoke up. "Leatherwood, maybe we'd better not do this. We were just supposed to bring her back, not kill anybody."

The leader's head jerked around. "This man's not going to tell me what to do. Our orders were to fetch the girl!"

"We'll be able to find her later." The man waved a hand at the landscape around them. "Where are they going to go that we can't find them whenever we want to? This is our home."

The one called Leatherwood hesitated. He glared back and forth between his companions and Conrad. "Elder Hissop was clear about what we're supposed to do. I don't know about you, Kiley, but I don't much want to go back without doin' as we were told."

"They won't get away," Kiley said. "Besides, after these men have been saddled with that head-strong female for a while, they may want us to take her off their hands!"

Leatherwood nodded. "That's a good point." He turned back to Conrad. "All right, mister, if you want her, take her. But know that by defyin' us, you've signed your death warrant. Sooner or later we'll kill you, and the girl will go back where she belongs."

17

"Talk like that makes me wonder why I don't just go ahead and drill you right now," Conrad said.

The squint-eyed Leatherwood grinned, which made him even uglier. "You're welcome to go ahead and try, mister."

Conrad began backing his horse away. Without taking his eyes off the six men, he raised his voice and said, "Arturo, take the girl and get out of here. I'll cover your back trail."

The Mormon gunmen stayed where they were. Conrad understood why the one called Kiley hadn't wanted to force the issue at that time. Outnumbered, surrounded by miles and miles of nothing, and no place where they could get any help, he and Arturo were at a definite disadvantage. The avenging angels could stalk them at their leisure, and Conrad and Arturo would have no way of knowing when or where the inevitable attack would come.

For now, more gunplay appeared to have been headed off, and Conrad had a chance to find out who the girl was and what was going on. He didn't mind fighting, but generally liked to know what he was fighting *for*, especially when trouble was delaying him in his efforts to find his missing children.

He heard the buggy and the girl's horse departing behind him, and continued backing his horse away from the gunmen. When he had

18

put a hundred yards between himself and them, he whirled the horse without warning and kicked it into a run. As he galloped after Arturo and the girl, he looked over his shoulder and saw the Mormons weren't giving chase. That surprised him a little, but obviously Leatherwood had decided they were going to bide their time.

Conrad was sure of one thing: the trouble was far from over.

Because Kiley was right. There was no place for them to go where the avenging angels couldn't find them.

Chapter 3

Conrad, Arturo, and their unexpected companion didn't stop until they had gone at least a mile. Conrad kept checking behind them. He was ready to stop and throw up a screen of rifle fire to cover their getaway, but the gunmen didn't come after them.

When they finally reined in, the horses were fatigued by the hard run. The young woman's horse was in the worst shape. She had been fleeing from her pursuers before Conrad and Arturo joined the chase.

She wasn't in much better shape. Trying to dismount, she half fell out of the saddle and had to grab hold of a stirrup to keep herself from dropping to the ground.

Conrad had already slid his Winchester into the saddle boot and swung down from the black. He reached out to grasp her arm and steady her. "Arturo," he said, "get one of the canteens."

Arturo turned around on the buggy seat, found a canteen in their boxes and bags of supplies, and brought the water over to them. Conrad unscrewed the cap and held the canteen to the young woman's mouth. She grabbed it with both hands and gulped down as much water as she could, but Conrad pulled the canteen away after a couple swallows.

"Take it easy," he told her. "You'll make yourself sick."

"I . . . I . . . Thank you," she gasped. "If you hadn't come along . . . I wouldn't have made it much farther."

While Conrad waited a moment before he gave her another drink, he took advantage of the opportunity to have a good look at her. She was tall and slender, and hair a little lighter in color than honey flowed all the way down her back to her hips. She wore men's clothing: a rough cotton shirt with the sleeves rolled up a couple turns on tanned forearms, brown twill trousers with suspenders that went over her shoulders, and work boots that laced up. Despite the clothing, no one would ever take her for anything but female.

"What's your name?" Conrad asked.

She'd been breathless when she dismounted, but she was starting to recover. "Selena. Selena Webster."

"I'm Conrad Browning. This is my friend Arturo Vincenzo."

Conrad handed her the canteen. She took a long drink but not enough to make her sick. As she gave him the canteen, she said, "I can't thank you enough for helping me, but I'm afraid you've just doomed yourselves. Like Jackson Leatherwood said, when you interfere with Father Agony's men, you've signed your own death warrant."

Despite the perilousness of their situation, Conrad laughed. "Father Agony?" he repeated. "That's a pretty melodramatic name, don't you think?"

Selena smiled, but there was no real humor in the expression. "That's what some of his wives call him. His name is Agonistes Hissop."

"The man's parents had odd taste in nomenclature," Arturo said.

"Or else they were readers and admirers of Milton's *Samson Agonistes*," Conrad said. "Agonistes being from Greek for 'one who struggles for a worthy cause.' "

Selena gave him an odd look. He didn't bother explaining he had taken a number of courses in the classics during his university days.

"The man's parents raised a monster," Selena

said after a moment. "His name is hardly the worst thing about him."

"He's the elder Leatherwood and who the others work for?" Conrad guessed.

Selena nodded. "He has a ranch about twenty miles northwest of here in a place called Juniper Canyon. It's more like his own little town, because a lot of his followers live there as well. He's a very rich, important man, and he doesn't let anyone forget it."

"You mentioned his . . . wives," Conrad said. "I seem to remember reading in the newspaper that the Mormon Church outlawed polygamy almost ten years ago."

That brought a laugh from Selena. "Just because Father Agony is a saint doesn't mean he agrees with everything the church leadership does. He believes he's a prophet, like Joseph Smith, and that God has granted him the wisdom and right to make his own laws. He's always had multiple wives, and he doesn't want to give them up."

Conrad nodded. "And let me guess . . . he wants to add you to the number?"

The grimace that momentarily twisted Selena's face was answer enough to that question. "I'll never marry him. He can kill me first, or more likely have Leatherwood and the rest of his avenging angels do it for him, but I don't care. That would be better than . . . than . . ."

"Maybe it won't come to that," Conrad said so

she wouldn't have to go on. "I don't like to brag, but Arturo and I are pretty good at handling trouble."

"Have you ever had an army of triggerites after you? Because that's what you'll be facing if you try to help me. I appreciate what you did, but you'd be better off if we went our separate ways. If Leatherwood and the others see that I'm not traveling with you, maybe he'll spare your lives. Maybe."

Conrad shook his head. "We're not going to abandon you. Once I take cards in a game, I like to play it out." He glanced toward the sun. "It's past the middle of the afternoon. We'll let the horses rest for a while longer, then we can start looking for a place to hole up for the night."

"Why don't you sit in the buggy, Miss Webster?" Arturo suggested. "The canopy provides a bit of shade from that brutal sun."

Selena smiled. "Thank you. You're very nice."

"Not really. I just know that having you suffer a sunstroke would only make our situation worse."

"Oh," she said. "Well, in that case, I appreciate it anyway." She climbed onto the buggy seat and heaved a weary sigh.

Conrad kept an eye not only on the area where they had left Jackson Leatherwood and the other avenging angels but also on the rest of the landscape around them. He wouldn't put it past Leatherwood and the others to circle around and come at them from a different direction. The vast expanse of Utah seemed as open and empty as if it had been on the moon.

Selena's exhaustion caught up to her, and she dozed off with her head sagging forward. While she was sleeping, Arturo asked Conrad, "Are you sure that getting involved in this young woman's problems is a good idea, sir?"

"No," Conrad said, "it's a terrible idea. We need to get on about our own business. I know that. But . . . look at her. She's not much more than a girl."

"A very attractive girl."

Conrad shrugged. "Yes, but that doesn't have anything to do with it. She's in trouble, and if we don't help her, who will? Maybe we can take her some place where she'll be safe from those men."

He didn't explain to Arturo how his dreams— and sometimes even his waking moments—had been haunted by Rebel for months after her death. Whenever he'd been faced by the decision of whether to help someone or just ride on, her sweet voice had seemed to whisper in his ear that he had to help . . . because that's what *she* would have done. Rebel wasn't there anymore, but Conrad could honor the life she had led and the legacy she left behind by not turning his back on people who needed a hand.

Or in his case, a gun hand.

Half an hour later, Conrad tied Selena's horse

to the back of the buggy. Selena stirred when Arturo climbed onto the seat beside her. Suddenly her head snapped up and she looked around, wide-eyed with terror.

"It's all right, Miss Webster," Arturo told her. "You're among friends."

She looked like she wanted to bolt out of the buggy and take off running. After a moment, her fear seemed to subside, and she sank back onto the seat. "I'm sorry. At first I . . . I didn't remember what happened. I thought I'd passed out some-where and that Leatherwood and his men were still after me." Her laugh was edged with bitter-ness. "Which they still are, of course. They'll never give up. Not as long as they're alive." She looked back and forth between Conrad and Arturo. "Are you sure you want to take on my troubles?"

Conrad stepped up into the saddle. "We wouldn't have it any other way," he said with a smile.

Chapter 4

They made camp at the foot of a small mesa, giving them protection from the chilly winds that often sprang up at night. Conrad started to unsaddle Selena's horse before he tended to the black and the buggy team.

She hopped down from the buggy and hurried over. "I can take care of my horse. I don't want to be any more of a burden than I have to."

"I don't mind—"

"No, I'll handle it," she said as she unstrapped the saddlebags and set them aside. "I insist."

Conrad shrugged and turned to the black gelding. Obviously, Selena Webster was a proud young woman.

While it was still light, Arturo kindled a small and almost smokeless fire to boil coffee, fry bacon, and heat up some beans and biscuits left over from supper the night before. The fire would be out by the time the sun set. Conrad figured Leatherwood and the others wouldn't have much trouble tracking them, but it didn't make sense to help their enemies by announcing where they were.

Selena shook her head when Arturo offered her a cup of coffee. "I don't take stimulants. No offense."

"Oh, none taken," he assured her. "I *do* require stimulants, especially when traveling through a godforsaken wilderness. This way there's more for me."

Selena smiled. "It's not godforsaken. This part of Utah may not look like much, but God is here."

Conrad hunkered on his heels and reached for the cup Arturo offered him. "From the things you say, I suppose you're a Mormon, too."

"Of course. I never denied my faith, Mr.

Browning. Just because I don't want to marry Father Agony doesn't mean that I'm . . ."

Conrad smiled. "A heathen Gentile like me?"

"That's not exactly how I would have put it."

"Don't worry," Conrad told her. "I don't spend a lot of time worrying about anybody's religion, or lack of it, including my own. I'll admit to being curious, though. Were you raised out here?"

Selena nodded as she took the tin plate Arturo handed her. "That's right. My grandparents on both sides came here with Brigham Young. My family has been here ever since."

"What about your parents? Do they live at this Juniper Canyon place?"

Selena's mouth tightened. "My father does. My mother passed away a year ago."

"Condolences," Arturo murmured.

"My father is one of Father Agony's men," Selena continued. "Father Agony has had his eye on me ever since . . . well, ever since I stopped being a little girl. My mother knew I didn't want to marry him, so while she was still alive she was able to exert enough influence on my father to keep him dragging his feet on the matter whenever Father Agony approached him. But since she passed on . . . I knew it was just a matter of time before my father agreed to what Father Agony wants. He'll make it worthwhile for my father."

"I have to say I mean no offense, Miss Webster,

27

but bartering one's flesh and blood that way seems rather medieval," Arturo commented. "Even barbaric."

"It's the way things are done at Juniper Canyon, and in other places, too," Selena said with a fatalistic tone in her voice. "And it's not always bad. Some of the elders are fine men, and their wives are very happy. I just don't want to live my life that way."

"Nobody can blame you for that," Conrad said. "And nobody should force you to, either."

"Unfortunately, they can do that, whether it's legal or not. They're a law unto themselves." Selena looked off across the plains. "I thought if I could get away from there, I'd go to California. I might be safe there."

"How do you plan on getting there?"

"I . . . I have a little money. My mother saved it. She meant to use it to help me get away when the time came, and she told me where she hid it. And that horse is mine. My father gave it to me. I didn't steal it."

Conrad shook his head. "I never said you did."

"I know." Selena cast her eyes down. "I'm sorry. I'm used to everyone being suspicious of me all the time."

"Perhaps with good reason," Arturo put in, "since you *did* run away."

"All I know is that I'm not going back," Selena said with more than a touch of defiance. "They'll have to kill me to get me back to Juniper Canyon, and I don't think Father Agony would be very happy about that."

"It's not going to come to that," Conrad said. "It just so happens we're headed west. You'll come along with us, and when we get into Nevada and find a town, we can put you on a train for San Francisco. The men who are after you will have a pretty hard time finding you there. We might even come across a flag stop along the way and manage to get you on a train before we get to Nevada."

"That would be wonderful! Like I said, I can pay—"

"Don't worry about that. You'll need your money once you get to California."

"But you've already done so much—"

"It won't be a problem," Conrad assured her.

Through various companies and holdings he owned a considerable amount of stock in the Southern Pacific, and in a number of other railroad lines as well. In fact, due to his half of the business empire he had inherited from his mother, Conrad Browning was one of the richest men in the country. The only less likely tycoon was probably his father Frank Morgan, who had never let his newfound wealth change him one little bit from the drifting gunfighter he had been for decades.

The sun was a red ball touching the tops of the

mountains. As soon as it dropped below the peaks, night would fall with stunning swiftness. "We'd better put the fire out before it gets dark," Conrad told Arturo.

While Arturo was doing that, Conrad checked on the horses picketed nearby. As soon as the light faded, he intended to saddle the animals again, in case they needed to get away in a hurry during the night. In fact, he decided, it might be a good idea to take more precautions than that. Leatherwood or one of the other avenging angels might have been watching them from a distance with field glasses.

Selena looked drowsy. She'd had a bedroll strapped behind her saddle, and Conrad figured she'd like to curl up in it and get some sleep. But those precautions he had thought of came first.

He went back to kneel beside the extinguished fire and said quietly, "As soon as it's dark, we're going to move camp."

"Why?" Selena asked. "This seems like a good place."

"Yeah, and those fellas who are after you might think so, too. They may have been watching without us knowing. If they think this is where we're camped, they're liable to slip in here and grab you during the night."

A shudder ran through her at Conrad's words. "I understand. I don't want that to happen."

"Neither do we."

As Conrad expected, night descended quickly. The sky faded from blue to black, with millions of stars seeming to wink into existence. The floor of the desert was cloaked in stygian gloom.

Working by feel, Conrad and Arturo hitched the team to the buggy. Conrad intended to saddle Selena's horse for her, but by the time they were finished with the buggy, she had already taken care of that chore. Conrad turned his attention to the black gelding.

When they were ready to go, he said quietly, "We'll lead the horses at a slow walk to keep from making as much noise as we can. Sounds carry a long way out here."

"I know," Selena said. "I grew up here, remember?"

"Then maybe you know of some other place we can camp."

She thought about it for a moment, then said, "If I'm right about where we are, there are some big rocks about two miles from here."

"Can you find them in the dark?"

"Maybe. They should be west of us. I know a little about steering by the stars."

"So do I," Conrad said. "Let's go."

Chapter 5

Conrad listened for the sound of horses moving around the countryside as he, Arturo, and Selena led the animals at a deliberate pace toward the rocks Selena had mentioned. He didn't hear anything except the steady hoofbeats of their horses and the faint sighing of the night wind. If Leatherwood and the rest of the Mormon gunmen were on the move, they were probably trying to be quiet about it, too.

When they had gone what seemed like two miles, Selena whispered, "I don't understand. We should have found the rocks by now."

"They're around here somewhere," Conrad told her. "If you get off line just a little, it can make a big difference in where you end up. Let's stop here and take a look around."

They halted and spread out to scan the surrounding landscape as best they could by starlight. After a moment, Arturo said, "I think I see something."

Conrad and Selena joined him, and he pointed toward some dark shapes in the distance. "Could that be them?"

"I think it is," Selena said.

With a specific destination in sight, they set off again, and a few minutes later found themselves standing in front of the scattered slabs of rock, the largest of which were ten feet tall and thirty feet wide.

"What a distinctive formation," Arturo said. "If I were a geologist, I think I might like to study these rocks."

"If you were a geologist, you probably wouldn't be here," Conrad pointed out.

"I didn't think I was a two-fisted, gun-totin' frontiersman, either, but sometimes fate forces us into strange and unexpected roles."

Conrad laughed. "That's certainly true. The two of you ought to be all right here. I'm going back to the mesa."

"Back to the mesa?" Selena repeated. "Why in the world would you do that if you think Leatherwood and his men might attack the camp we had there?"

"While it was still light I noticed a little trail leading to the top. If I can get up there, I'll hear them when they ride up and maybe I can eavesdrop on whatever they say. It could give us a real advantage if we know what their plans are."

"That's a very astute observation and a cunning stratagem," Arturo said. "I'll stand guard here, I assume?"

"That's the plan," Conrad said.

"Very good. Be careful, sir."

"Yes." Selena moved closer to Conrad in the darkness. She reached out and rested her hand on his arm for a second. "Be careful. I really don't want you getting killed on my account."

"I don't intend to," Conrad said.

He took his Winchester but left his horse, heading off on foot back in the direction they had come from. He moved at an easy trot that ate up the ground but was almost noiseless.

Lit by the faint, silvery glow of the stars, the landscape around him was eerie, and once again Conrad was struck by how alien his surroundings were, as if he were on some other planet. At times he felt like the only human presence in a vast emptiness.

But that wasn't true, of course. Other humans were out there in the darkness, and unfortunately, they wanted him dead.

He was going to do his very best to disappoint them.

His sense of direction didn't betray him. The mesa where he and Arturo and Selena had camped briefly loomed up ahead of him. He paused to listen but didn't hear men or animals moving around anywhere. Hoping he wasn't headed right into a trap, he resumed trotting toward the mesa.

When he reached it, he had to hunt around for a few minutes before he found the trail he had noticed earlier. It was a rough ledge barely wide enough for one man that wound around the mesa. The footing was treacherous. Taking it slow he climbed toward the top. At one point a rock rolled under his foot, nearly throwing him off balance. The mesa wasn't that tall, seventy or eighty feet maybe, but a fall from the ledge might prove fatal. At the very least he would be hurt badly enough to be easy prey for Leatherwood and his avenging angels.

The climb took several minutes, but when Conrad reached the top he could see for a long way all around. During the day the view would extend for miles.

The mesa was about a hundred yards in diameter. A few bushes grew on top, but mostly the vegetation consisted of clumps of grass. Conrad stretched out not far from the edge over-looking the spot where their camp had been. From there he could also cover the top of the trail. If Leatherwood and the other gunmen discovered he was up there, they would have him trapped. There was nowhere for him to go unless he sprouted wings and flew away. But, they would have to come up that ledge one at a time, and he could pick them off with ease. They would have to starve him out—

Which they might be perfectly capable of doing. Conrad wouldn't be surprised at all if they were that merciless.

The ground retained some of the day's warmth, even though the sun had set several hours earlier, but the night breezes sweeping the top of the mesa grew increasingly chilly. Conrad didn't mind. The cool air helped keep him awake.

His senses were attuned to his surroundings, but he knew his hearing was the most valuable. In all likelihood he would hear the approach of the gunmen before he saw them . . . assuming they showed up at all.

The minutes dragged past. He wasn't sure how long he had been waiting, but thought the moon ought to be rising any time. If Leatherwood was going to make a move, it would have to be soon.

A few moments later, he heard a faint, almost indiscernible *clink!*—the sound of metal hitting rock—someone's spur, a gun barrel, something like that. It was enough to tell him someone was out there. Silently, he crawled forward until he could look over the mesa's rim.

Suddenly, orange flame burst out below him. The glare was blindingly bright to eyes long accustomed to darkness. He jerked his head down and squeezed his eyes closed, hoping his night vision hadn't been completely ruined.

During that fleeting instant when the fire seemed to fill his sight, he caught a glimpse of the blazing brand—a bundle of sagebrush or greasewood—as it flew through the air toward the campsite. He thought whoever had thrown it had two reasons for doing so. He wanted to blind and disorient the people who were supposed to be camping there . . .

And he wanted some light to shoot by.

That was confirmed a second later when a harsh voice shouted, "Hold your fire, hold your fire! They're not here!"

Jackson Leatherwood. Conrad was sure of it. The leader of the avenging angels had brought his men to wipe out Conrad and Arturo and recapture Selena Webster, but the plan had come up empty.

The bundle of burning brush lay on the ground near the foot of the cliff. Ominous shapes moved out of the darkness and into the edge of the circle of light cast by the flames. Conrad recognized the wide-brimmed hats and the long coats. He even got a look at Leatherwood's scarred face as the man strode forward and angrily kicked the burning brush apart, scattering it and causing sparks to fly in the air.

"They didn't make camp here after all," Leatherwood said. "They must have eaten supper and moved on."

"But I saw them," one of the men whined. "They unsaddled their horses, unhitched the team from the buggy, and spread their bedrolls."

"Tricks!" Leatherwood raged. "Tricks meant to fool you—and they did!"

"I'm sorry, Jackson," the man muttered.

Leatherwood stomped around a little more, letting off steam. "The closest good water is in the tanks at Frenchman's Flat. They'll have to head there or the water stop on the railroad at Navajo Wash. We'll split up. Kiley, take two of the men and ride to the wash. The rest of us will go to Frenchman's Flat."

"Are you sure it's a good idea dividing our forces like that, Jackson?" Kiley asked. His voice, along with those of the others, was crystal clear to Conrad on top of the mesa.

"There were only two men," Leatherwood snapped.

"Plus the girl. That makes three. The odds are even if you count her."

"She's a girl. She's not going to fight."

"She had the gumption to run away from Elder Hissop," Kiley pointed out. "She might surprise you."

"Let's get back to the horses," Leatherwood said. "God is on our side. He's not going to take the side of a couple Gentiles and a wayward girl over His own avenging angels."

Conrad hoped Leatherwood was wrong about that.

In order to keep dodging trouble until they got out of the reach of those fanatical gunmen, he and Arturo and Selena could use all the help they could get, divine or otherwise.

Chapter 6

Conrad waited while the men walked off and vanished into the darkness. They were no longer trying to be quiet, so he was able to hear their footsteps. A few minutes later, the swift rataplan of hoofbeats drifted to his ears as the avenging angels rode away from the mesa.

He waited until he couldn't hear the horses at all, then waited some more. Finally satisfied the gunmen were gone, he stood up, made his way to the ledge, and started down.

As he climbed he thought about what to do next. He and Arturo had several canteens full of water, as well as a small barrel of it stowed in the back of the buggy, but it was a long, dry stretch across that part of Utah. Conrad had planned to take advantage of the water stops along the railroad.

He'd just learned some of their enemies would be waiting for them at Navajo Wash, so that was out. And so were the tanks at Frenchman's Flat, wherever that was. Maybe Selena would know of another place they could replenish their water supply.

When he reached the bottom of the trail, he turned in the direction of the rocks, but had taken only a couple steps before he heard an all-too-familiar sound behind him—the ugly, metallic ratcheting of a gun being cocked.

A hard voice immediately followed. "Don't move, mister. It'll be easier on me keeping you alive, but I'll shoot you if I have to."

Conrad froze. He recognized the voice. "Kiley."

"You know me?"

"Only by what Leatherwood called you. I thought you went to Navajo Wash."

"I know what you thought," Kiley said with a note of boastful pride. "I told the other men with me to go on, that I'd catch up to them at the wash, then doubled back here on foot. I spotted that little ledge when we were here earlier. Jackson never noticed it, but I thought at least one of you might be on top of the mesa. Looks like I was right. I would have gone up, but I heard you coming down and decided to wait and get the drop on you."

"You want all the credit for bringing back the girl, don't you? You're trying to impress Father Agony so he'll make you the top man in his gang."

Conrad heard the sharp, angry hiss of breath between Kiley's teeth. "Don't you disrespect Elder Hissop by using that awful name for him. You shouldn't refer to the avenging angels as a gang, either. We're doing the Lord's work."

"By killing?"

"If that's what it takes. Now tell me, are the other two still up there?"

"I'm not telling you anything."

"Then you're a fool. I'll put a bullet in your knee so you can't run and you'll hurt so bad you'll tell me anything I want to know. Or you can cooperate, and once I have the girl, I'll let you and your friend go."

Normally Conrad wouldn't have believed a promise like that. He didn't know Mormons well enough to be sure what they might do, however. Maybe Kiley was telling the truth.

It didn't really matter. Conrad wasn't going to turn Selena over to him. No matter how Agonistes Hissop's other wives felt about it, Selena regarded marriage to the elder as being locked away in prison, and Conrad wasn't going to condemn her to that.

His mind raced furiously. His options were limited. In the bad light he might be able to throw himself to the side, whirl around, and drill Kiley with a round from the Winchester before the man could shoot him. But Kiley would get at least one shot off, and the sound of the blasts would travel a long way over the desert. Leatherwood and the rest of the avenging angels would hear them and likely come galloping back.

He decided for the moment the best thing to do was stall and wait for an opportunity. "All right," he said with a defeated sigh. "They're waiting up there while I check things out down here. You can go up and see for yourself."

"And turn my back on you?" Kiley laughed. "I don't think so. You go up the trail first."

Conrad didn't know Kiley, but the gunman didn't know him, either. He had no idea Conrad Browning would never give in so easily.

"All right," he said as he started toward the ledge, dropping the Winchester. "Just be careful with that gun. I don't want you shooting me accidentally."

"If I shoot you, it won't be by accident."

Conrad stepped onto the ledge. He kept his hands in plain sight so Kiley wouldn't get nervous and trigger-happy. In some places the path was so steep and rough he had to rest his left hand on the mesa wall to steady himself. He heard Kiley breathing hard a few steps behind him.

If he climbed all the way to the top Kiley would realize Arturo and Selena weren't there. He would be in the same position he'd been in when Kiley first got the drop on him. Conrad needed to turn the tables on the gunman.

Recognizing the spot where he'd almost lost his balance Conrad stepped over the rock in the trail. Planting his foot, he kicked back. His boot heel hit the rock and sent it rolling down the trail right under Kiley's feet.

The gunman let out a startled yell. As Conrad

swung around, he saw that dodging the rock had caused Kiley to lose his balance and fling out both arms to catch himself, which meant the gun in his hand wasn't pointed at Conrad anymore.

Lunging at the man Conrad reached out to close his hand over the revolver's cylinder so the hammer would strike the web of flesh between his thumb and forefinger rather than the bullet in the chamber. In the same movement he swung a hard punch at Kiley's head, intending to knock Kiley off the ledge and send him plummeting to the hard ground forty feet below. At the very least, a fall like that would injure the gunman enough to render him harmless for a while.

Kiley jerked his head aside as the glancing blow scraped over his ear. Trying to wrestle his revolver out of Conrad's grip he lowered his shoulder and bulled into him, slamming him against the mesa's sandstone wall.

Neither man said anything as they struggled on the narrow ledge. Kiley got a hand on Conrad's throat and forced him toward the edge. Conrad planted his feet and jabbed a punch into Kiley's midsection. The thought crossed Conrad's mind that they might both topple off the ledge and fall to their deaths.

He grabbed hold of Kiley's duster and pulled himself closer. His knee came up, aimed at the gunman's groin. Kiley twisted aside and took the blow on his thigh. He tightened his grip on

Conrad's throat and drove Conrad's head against the rock with stunning force that made sky-rockets explode inside his skull.

As he fought to hold on to consciousness, Conrad threw his strength into another heave on the revolver and finally ripped it free of Kiley's grasp. Slashing at the gunman's head he felt the butt thud heavily against Kiley's temple. Kiley groaned in pain and his grip on Conrad's throat loosened. Conrad took the advantage and knocked Kiley's hand away from him. For a split second, neither of them had hold of the other.

Conrad pressed his back against the mesa and lifted his right foot in a kick that landed in Kiley's belly. Kiley bent over and stumbled back a step, his right foot sliding off the edge of the trail. He yelled and flung his hands out toward the wall in a frantic scrabble for a grip that would save him, but there was nothing there. His arms windmilled futilely as he pitched to the side, away from the mesa. Then he was gone, falling through the darkness as a scream ripped from his throat.

That scream lasted only a second before an ugly thud abruptly silenced it. Conrad stood with his back against the wall, his chest heaving as he tried to catch his breath. His head was still spinning from being rammed against the rock.

After a few moments, he felt steady enough to straighten and look over the trail's edge. He saw a dark, unmoving shape sprawled on the ground.

With Kiley's unfired gun in his hand, he went back down the trail, moving as quickly as he dared. When he reached the bottom, he kept the revolver leveled at Kiley's motionless form. As he approached he saw a spreading pool of black under the gunman's head. Kiley must have landed on a rock that split his skull wide open, Conrad thought.

He risked checking for a pulse and found none. Kiley was dead. He would do no more avenging for Elder Agonistes Hissop.

Conrad straightened from that grim task and tucked Kiley's gun behind his belt. Sooner or later the two men on their way to Navajo Wash would wonder why Kiley hadn't caught up with them.

That meant he had a chance to surprise them, Conrad realized. He had to find Kiley's horse. The animal couldn't be too far away. He stripped the duster off the dead man, picked up Kiley's hat, and then headed off into the darkness.

Chapter 7

Conrad headed in the direction of Navajo Wash and found the gunman's horse tied to a mesquite about half a mile from the mesa. He unfastened the reins and led the animal toward the big rocks.

He had left on foot and was coming back with a horse, so he wasn't surprised when Arturo called out, "Whoever you are, stop right there! I have a rifle pointed at you, and I'm not afraid to use it!"

"It's me, Arturo," Conrad called back. "I'm coming in."

He trotted the rest of the way to the camp in the rocks, where Arturo and Selena greeted him with questions. "Where did you get the horse?" Arturo asked. Selena followed by saying, "Are you all right?"

"I'm fine," Conrad assured her, then turned to Arturo. "The horse belonged to that fellow Kiley who was with Leatherwood earlier."

"Belonged?" Arturo repeated. "As in, the individual is now dead?"

"That pretty much sums it up."

Selena said, "We didn't hear any shots."

"There weren't any." Quickly, Conrad explained how Leatherwood and the other avenging angels had sneaked up on the mesa only to find their quarry gone, then discussed their plans while Conrad was eavesdropping on them. "I thought they were all gone, but when I got down to the bottom of the trail, Kiley was waiting for me. He had doubled back on foot."

"And you killed him without firing a shot?" Selena sounded amazed. "How on earth did you manage that?"

Conrad told them about the fight on the ledge.

"It was pretty close to a disaster," he concluded, "but I was finally able to get the upper hand."

"Along with the man's horse and gun," Arturo said.

"That's not all." Conrad had draped Kiley's duster over the saddle and hung the gunman's hat on the saddlehorn. He took them down and went on, "If I was wearing these and riding this horse, from a distance I could pass for Kiley."

"And there are only two men at this place called Navajo Wash," Arturo said, proving he had caught on to what Conrad was talking about.

"Exactly. If they think it's Kiley riding up on them, they won't be looking for trouble."

"Wait a minute," Selena said. "What is it you're planning on doing, Mr. Browning? Riding in and shooting it out with those men?"

"Not necessarily. If I can get close enough without them realizing who I am, I can disarm them, tie them up, and leave them there for Leatherwood to find when he realizes we're not going to Frenchman's Flat. That plan depends on a couple things, though. Are you familiar with this Navajo Wash place?"

Selena nodded. "Elder Hissop had driven some of his cattle there to load them on the train when he sold them and had to ship them out. Sometimes practically the entire community would go along on those trips."

"Is there anything there except a water tank

so the locomotives can refill their boilers?"

"There's a siding and a little shed. That's all I recall. There's certainly not a settlement or anything like that."

Conrad nodded. "Then there won't be anybody around to help them or get caught in a crossfire."

"You mean no one will be in danger except you."

Conrad shrugged. "I have a pretty good idea what I'm getting into."

"So you're going to risk your life—again!— for someone you haven't even known for twelve hours."

"He does this sort of thing all the time," Arturo said.

"Why don't you let me worry about that?" Conrad suggested. "The next question is, do you know how to get to Navajo Wash from here?"

Selena hesitated, then said, "I think I can find it."

"In the dark?"

"Probably. It's on the railroad, so all we really have to do is find the tracks."

"How long will it take to get there?"

"I don't really know. A couple hours, maybe?"

The moon had risen while Conrad was on his way back to the rocks. He took out his watch, opened it, and used the moonlight to see the time. With a snap, he closed the watch.

"Try to get some sleep," he told Selena. "We

48

won't leave here for a while. I want to get to Navajo Wash before dawn, but when it's light enough so the men who are there can see me coming and recognize Kiley's coat and horse. The two of you will be well behind me, out of sight."

"I don't like it," Selena said, "but there's not really any point in arguing with you, is there?"

Arturo answered that question. "None at all."

Conrad was able to snatch an hour's sleep while Arturo stood watch, but his nerves were too taut to let him relax much. Everyone was still tired when they saddled the horses, hitched up the buggy team, and started for Navajo Wash.

Selena had insisted on saddling her own horse again, and Conrad was starting to think there was something odd about that. He didn't know what to make of it, but didn't want to press Selena for answers. He had more important things to worry about.

Selena seemed worried, too. From the seat of the buggy where she was riding, she asked, "Why can't we just go around Navajo Wash and avoid Frenchman's Flat, too?"

"If we don't stop at either of those places, where's the next good water?" Conrad asked as he rode alongside the vehicle.

She was slow in answering. "I don't know."

"Neither do I. That's the point. In country like this, you're better off taking on water wherever you can, because you don't know how long it'll be before you find more. There's something else to consider, too. It's possible a westbound train will come along while we're there, and we can get you on it without having to take you to Nevada. You could be out of this Father Agony's reach in a few hours."

"That sounds good," Selena admitted. "But we have no way of knowing a train will come along and stop there."

"It's a chance," Conrad agreed, "but I think it's a risk we can afford to run if we take care of those two men who are waiting there."

Selena started to say something else, but fell silent before the words left her mouth. Conrad had a pretty good idea what she was thinking. She was afraid of the avenging angels and didn't want them taking her back to Juniper Canyon, but they were also part of the community in which she had grown up. Conrad had killed one of them already, and two more of them might die at his hands before the sun came up. It had to bother her.

She didn't want to go back and marry Hissop. That feeling was the stronger, Conrad sensed. So she was torn. When it came down to making a choice, she would choose her freedom over the lives of the men pursuing her.

Nobody could blame her for that.

They practically tripped over the steel rails of the Southern Pacific. "Navajo Wash should be a few miles west of here," Selena said. "You'll cross the wash itself on a trestle before you get to the water tank. You'll be able to see the tank without any trouble."

"And the men waiting there should be able to see me," Conrad said as he looked at the eastern sky, which had started to turn gray with the approach of dawn. Sunrise was still an hour or so away. That would give him plenty of time to reach the wash before the sky brightened enough to give the waiting gunmen a good look at him.

He swung down from the black and tossed his Stetson into the back of the buggy. Arturo handed him Kiley's wider-brimmed hat. Conrad settled it on his head, then shrugged into the long duster they had brought with them.

"From a distance, you'll look enough like him to fool them," Arturo said with a satisfied nod.

"That's the idea." Conrad untied Kiley's dun from the back of the buggy.

Selena jumped to the ground and went over to him. "I've only known you for a few hours, and already this is the second time I'm telling you to be careful and not get killed."

"You might as well get used to it," Arturo put in.

Conrad smiled. "I'll be all right," he told Selena. "When they see me coming, they'll think I'm Kiley and they'll wonder where I've been all night. They'll be too curious to start shooting until it's too late."

"I hope you're right."

Conrad turned to Arturo. "I'll come back and get you when it's safe. Until then, stay here and keep your eyes open. Keep your Winchester handy, too."

"Like it's my oldest, dearest friend," Arturo promised.

Conrad mounted up, nodded to them, and heeled Kiley's horse into motion. The dun was a big, strong animal, and soon it stretched its legs into a smooth, ground-eating lope.

Conrad followed the twin dark lines of the rails as they arrowed westward. Arturo, Selena, and the buggy were soon out of sight behind him, disappearing into the thick gray predawn gloom. A cold wind swept the arid landscape.

Half an hour later, the sky was light enough that Conrad was able to spot something sticking up beside the tracks about half a mile ahead of him. He slowed the dun to a walk. Within a few minutes, he recognized the shape as a big round water tank elevated on a spidery framework of wooden legs. An eerie creaking sound drifted to his ears. After a second, he identified it as the blades turning on the adjacent windmill that pumped water from deep under the ground into the tank.

Conrad maintained his slow, steady approach. He came to the wash, a dry, wide, shallow cut in the ground that once or twice a year would fill with raging water during the flash floods caused by an occasional downpour making its way through the normally arid landscape. A trestle spanned the wash. Conrad rode onto it. The dun's shoes clinked against the cinders of the road-bed as the horse picked its way along, putting its hooves down between the crossties.

Conrad looked intently at the shed next to the water tank. He didn't see any movement, but it was big enough the two avenging angels and their horses could be concealed behind it. If they were there, likely they had spotted him already. They would be watching—ready for trouble—trying to make out his identity.

The dun reached the end of the trestle. Conrad moved the horse to the side of the rails again and urged it into a slightly faster pace. He was ready to get it over with, no matter how it played out.

The water tank was about a hundred yards beyond the wash. Conrad had covered half that distance when he saw two men step out from behind the shed, just as he expected. They were holding rifles, but as he tensed, poised to reach for his own Winchester which he had slipped into Kiley's saddle boot, one of the men suddenly took off his hat and waved it over his head in what Conrad took to be an all-clear signal. His heart thudded in his chest as he rode closer. His masquerade had worked, at least so far.

Only twenty yards more.

The man waving his hat clapped it back on his head and called, "Hey, Kiley, where have you been? We expected you a long time ago!"

The other man moved a step closer and asked a question of his own. "Did you run into trouble?"

Conrad didn't answer. He just kept the horse moving and narrowed the gap between him and the avenging angels that much more. He was almost in handgun range. . . .

The second man stopped short, shouted, "That's not Kiley!" and jerked his rifle to his shoulder. Flame spouted from the weapon's muzzle.

Chapter 8

Conrad dug his heels into the horse's flanks and sent the animal lunging ahead in a gallop. He heard the high-pitched whine of the rifle bullet pass his ear. The wind caught the wide-brimmed hat, plucked it from his head, and sent it sailing behind him. The long tails of the duster flapped like the wings of a giant bird.

The second whipcrack of a rifle sounded before the first shot had a chance to echo across the desert. Conrad didn't know where the slug went, but didn't feel its smashing impact. He drew his Colt and felt the familiar buck of its recoil against his palm as he triggered two swift shots.

The first man spun off his feet as those bullets crashed into him. Kiley's horse was practically on top of the second man, who leaped desperately out of the way to avoid being trampled and in the process dodged the shot Conrad sent toward him. The gunman dropped his rifle as he rolled, but he came up with his revolver in his fist, spitting fire. He threw three shots at Conrad as he made a dash for the shed.

Conrad didn't want the man to get behind cover. He fired again, but just as he squeezed the trigger, one of the man's wild shots burned across the dun's rump and made the horse leap in the air. He wasn't expecting that, and felt himself leaving the saddle. Quickly he kicked his feet free of the stirrups so the dun wouldn't drag him if it bolted.

He hit the ground hard enough to knock the wind out of him, but there was no time to rest and catch his breath. He forced his muscles to work and surged to his feet. A bullet kicked up grit and gravel just to his right. He snapped a shot at the remaining gunman, who was crouched at the corner of the shed.

Conrad was in a bad spot, and he knew it. He usually carried the Colt's hammer on an empty chamber, but had slipped a sixth round into the cylinder before he approached the water tank. He had one shot left in the revolver, his rifle was in the saddle boot on the horse that was kicking around twenty yards away, still spooked by that bullet burn on its rump, and the man who wanted to kill him had the only good cover anywhere around.

Well, maybe not the *only* cover, Conrad realized. The legs of the water tank were better than nothing. If he could make it up the ladder to the platform on which the tank sat, he could take cover behind the massive container. He broke into a run toward the tank and flung his last shot at the gunman. The bullet smacked into the shed wall close enough to make the man jerk back, giving Conrad a couple seconds.

He took advantage of the respite and ran as hard as he could. The framework of the tank's legs loomed in front of him, looking more spider-like than ever in the dim light. A slug chewed splinters from one of the thick beams as Conrad ducked behind them. He pouched the empty iron and reached as high as he could on the ladder. Another bullet whistled past his head as he started to climb.

He almost lost his hold on the ladder as he felt the vibration of a bullet hitting one of the rungs he was grasping. A splinter stung his cheek—but he didn't fall. He kept moving, and a second later he reached the top and hauled himself onto the platform. A fast roll and jump put him behind the tank itself. The thick wood, and the thousands of gallons of water they held, would shield him from any more bullets.

But a standoff wasn't what he wanted. As he lay there he pulled fresh cartridges from the loops on his shell belt and thumbed them into the Colt, filling the cylinder again. He couldn't afford to let the gunman pin him down. Arturo and Selena were waiting for him to return. He had to dispose of the last avenging angel so they could fill their canteens and water barrel, then wait for a train to come along or head west again, depending on what else happened.

The gunman had stopped shooting at him. In the echoing silence, the man shouted, "Hey! You hear me, mister?"

Conrad didn't see what harm it would do to answer. "I hear you!"

"Where's Kiley? How'd you get his horse and clothes?"

"Think about it," Conrad said. "Even a hard-case like you ought to be able to come up with the answer!"

"You—" The man bit off whatever he'd been about to say. Evidently he took his religion seriously enough that he wasn't going to curse, no matter how angry he was. "You shouldn't have done that, mister."

"And you shouldn't be trying to kidnap an innocent young woman!"

"You don't know our ways! You got no right to interfere! Elder Hissop's a prophet, same as Joseph Smith or Brigham Young! He's one of the anointed of God! You can't oppose his will!" A bark of harsh laughter came from the man. "Anyway, you can't call that shameless jezebel an innocent young woman! If that's what you think, you're a fool!"

Conrad didn't know and didn't care what the man meant by that. He was trying to figure out some way of ending the standoff before it dragged on much longer.

The shed was fairly close to the structure supporting the water tank. Ten feet separated them, Conrad judged. He looked at the tank itself. The pipe supplying the water ran up the side of the tank, then turned at a ninety-degree angle to go through an opening near the top. He thought he might be able to climb up that pipe, crawl over the cover on top used to keep the fierce heat of the Utah sun from evaporating the water it held, and leap down to the shed roof, which was almost flat and had only a slight slope to it.

Would the roof hold him, or would he crash through it and break a leg . . . or his neck?

He was fairly certain the gunman wouldn't expect him to try such a loco stunt. And that's what it was, no mistake about that. But if it worked, he could take the man completely by surprise and put an end to the impasse.

Once Conrad came up with a plan, he didn't spend a lot of time mulling it over or brooding about its chances of success. He didn't see any

58

other way out so he stood up and eased partway around the tank on the narrow platform until he came to the water pipe. There was just enough room between the pipe and the wall of the tank for him to get his fingers in there. He holstered the Colt, reached over his head, and grasped the pipe, hoping the braces attaching it to the tank were sturdy enough to support his weight.

He leaned back to test the pipe. It seemed strong, without any give to it. Conrad lifted his right leg and planted the sole of his boot against the side of the tank. The thick, curving planks were rough enough to give him a little purchase. The muscles in his arms and shoulders bunched as he hauled himself upward.

It was a hard climb, but the tank was only about ten feet tall, so it didn't take too long. As Conrad reached the top and rolled onto the boards, the man behind the shed called out to him again.

"What's it gonna be, mister? I can stay here all day and keep you up there. Pretty soon the sun will be up, and you won't have any shade. It'll fry you like an egg. Not only that, but Leatherwood and the rest of the men will be here before the day's over. We'll surround that water tank and pick you off. You might as well give up now."

Conrad didn't respond. He lay there a few minutes, letting the quivering muscles in his arms, shoulders, and back recover.

Without standing up, he peeled out of the duster

and left it lying on top of the tank. Then he crawled to the other side. He couldn't see the man who crouched at the edge of the shed. When he made his move, he wanted the gunman's attention focused elsewhere, so he reached in his pocket and slid out a silver dollar. With a flick of his wrist he sent the coin sailing over the railroad tracks. When the silver dollar landed on a crosstie, it bounced and struck one of the rails with a loud ringing sound.

That was enough to make the tightly-stretched nerves of the gunman snap. He whirled toward the sound and triggered his gun. Three shots roared out.

And while that gun thunder rolled, Conrad surged to his feet, drew his Colt, and left the top of the water tank in a leap that carried him toward the shed.

Chapter 9

For a breathtaking instant, Conrad seemed to hang in midair. Then his boots slammed down on the shed roof, his momentum carrying him forward, off the little building. He tucked himself into a roll as his feet hit the sandy ground behind the gunman. Twisting he came back up on one knee. The gunman turned toward him, but Conrad's gun was already level. Flame stabbed from the muzzle as he fired twice.

Both slugs slammed into the gunman's body and drove him back against the shed wall. His gun went off as his finger clenched convulsively on the trigger, but the weapon was pointed down and the bullet went harmlessly into the ground. He dropped his revolver and pitched forward, sprawling on his face.

Conrad sprang up and kicked the fallen Colt out of reach while he covered the man he had just shot.

The avenging angel didn't move. Working the toe of his boot under the man's shoulder Conrad rolled him onto his back. Reddish-gold light of the dawn reflected back from the man's sightless, staring eyes.

Just as Conrad reached down with his left hand to close the man's eyes, another shot blasted out. The bullet whipped through the air above his head. He threw himself forward on his belly and lifted his gun.

The first man he'd shot wasn't dead! The man's shirt was crimson with blood under the duster he wore, but he had managed to climb to his feet and stagger to the shed. The revolver in his hand roared again. Conrad fired at the same instant, the two shots sounding like one.

The gunman's bullet kicked up dirt inches from Conrad's shoulder. The bullet from Conrad's

Colt, traveling upward at an angle, caught the man just under the chin and bored into the base of his brain. More blood poured out over the man's chest as he staggered back a step, already dead even though his body hadn't quite caught up to that fact. Slowly, he crumpled to the ground.

Conrad climbed to his feet. He was the only one left alive at the isolated water stop.

He reloaded the Colt and slipped it back into the holster. The horses belonging to the two dead men were spooked by the shooting and gunsmoke, but they were tied securely behind the shed and weren't going anywhere. Kiley's horse stood off down the tracks, seeming to have calmed down after being grazed by that bullet. Conrad figured he and his companions would take all three of the horses with them. In the rugged country, having extra mounts could turn out to be very important.

His eyes narrowed as he caught sight of dust moving along the tracks to the east where he had left Arturo and Selena. Figuring Leatherwood and the other avenging angels might have found them, Conrad hurried toward Kiley's horse, talking softly in hopes the animal wouldn't shy away. He wanted the Winchester in the saddle boot.

The horse gave him a wall-eyed stare but didn't run. Conrad grabbed hold of the reins with his left hand and used his right to draw the rifle from its sheath. Moving quickly, he led the horse back to the shed and tied it with the other two. They knew Kiley's horse and nickered softly in welcome.

Conrad stepped to the corner of the shed and levered a round into the Winchester's firing chamber. Ready to bring the rifle to his shoulder and start shooting, he watched the cloud of dust come closer.

He began to make out the shape at the base of the cloud and grunted in surprise as he recognized the buggy. When the vehicle came closer he saw Arturo handling the team and Selena sitting beside him. Conrad didn't see anyone chasing them.

He stepped out from behind the shed so they could see him. As the buggy got closer, Arturo slowed the team and brought it to a halt. Conrad was a little surprised to see Selena holding Arturo's Winchester. He wondered if she would have used it if she'd needed to.

"Are you all right?" she called to him as she climbed down from the buggy.

"I'm fine," Conrad told her.

She turned toward him, and exclaimed, "My God, you're bleeding!"

Conrad reached up and touched his cheek. A single drop of blood was on his fingertip when he took it away.

"A flying splinter nicked me, that's all. I'm all right. The question is, what are you two doing here? You were supposed to wait for me to come back and get you."

"Tell that to the young lady," Arturo said. "We heard shots—"

"And then a few minutes later we heard more," Selena said. "I thought you might need our help."

"Miss Webster can be very persistent when she wants something," Arturo said, which Conrad thought was pretty ironic. Few people he had ever encountered could be more persistent—and annoying about it—than Arturo.

"Well, it's all over now, and I'm fine. Let's fill up those canteens and the water barrel while we've got the chance."

"The men who were waiting here . . ." Selena began.

Conrad leaned his head toward the shed. "Around on the other side. You don't want to go there."

"I'm sorry," she murmured. "I've caused so much trouble. Three men are dead because of me."

"That's where you're wrong. Those men are dead because they were willing to kill to do what that fellow Hissop wants. If you want to blame somebody, blame them, and him, not yourself."

"I . . . I know you're right. I just wish it had never come to this."

"So do I," Conrad said.

Arturo got the water barrel and the canteens out of the buggy while Conrad got hold of the chain attached to the spout leading from the tank.

"We're going to get wet," he warned Arturo. "These tanks are designed so locomotives can refill their boilers, not for putting water in smaller containers like these. If there was a station here, the railroad would've put in a hand pump and a spigot, but they figure something like that isn't necessary at a water stop."

Arturo tugged his derby down tighter on his head. "I'll be fine, sir." He stood on the tracks and held the barrel out in front of him. "Fill away."

Conrad tugged the chain to lower the spout, and water began to gush from it. The flow splashed over Arturo's head and splattered on Conrad. He called to Selena, "Come hold the chain while I help Arturo with the barrel!"

She was smiling as she came over to him, and he had to admit the sight of Arturo getting soaked was pretty amusing. A moment later he was in the same boat as he helped his friend hold the barrel under the pouring water. In moments they were both wet to the skin.

"Let it up!" Conrad told Selena when the barrel was almost full. After filling the canteens from the barrel, then refilling it to the top, he and Arturo carried it over to the buggy and placed it in the back. Arturo replaced the lid and tapped it down. Puddles of muddy water covered the ground, but it wouldn't take long for the sandy soil to soak them up.

"Now there's just one more thing to do," Conrad

said as he reached into the back of the buggy and got a short-handled shovel from their gear.

Selena's smile disappeared when she saw what Conrad was holding. "You carry a shovel with you?"

"You'd be surprised how often we have to bury someone," Arturo said.

Chapter 10

Conrad told Selena to watch for a train while he and Arturo attended to the grim task of burying the two gunmen behind the shed. He hadn't done that for Kiley, and he wouldn't have bothered for those two if he hadn't thought it might make Selena feel a little better if she knew the bodies hadn't been left for the buzzards.

At Conrad's suggestion, she climbed onto the platform and sat beside the water tank where she could look up and down the tracks. He told her to check the other directions from time to time as they still had to worry about Leatherwood and the men who had gone to Frenchman's Flat showing up.

Conrad was tamping down the dirt he'd replaced in the grave shared by the two avenging angels when Selena called, "I think I see something coming! It might be a train!"

Conrad tossed the shovel to Arturo to put back in the buggy, and climbed up to join Selena on the platform. She pointed along the tracks to the east where puffs of smoke could be seen in the far distance.

"Looks like a locomotive, all right," he said. "And it's even headed in the right direction. It's still several miles away."

"Maybe it won't stop here." Hope and worry mingled in Selena's voice.

"Chances are it will. I can't imagine an engineer passing up a chance to take on water in country like this."

At that moment, Arturo called from below in an alarmed voice, "Riders coming from the south!"

Conrad bit back a curse and hurried around the tank so he could look in that direction. Arturo was right. A dust cloud swirled into the air.

Selena came around the tank to join Conrad. "It's Leatherwood! It has to be."

Conrad thought she was probably right. It was going to be a tight race to see who arrived at the water stop first. The riders were closer, but the train was moving faster. Conrad figured there was a good chance everybody would get there about the same time.

He urged Selena toward the ladder. "You and Arturo get in the buggy and get ready to head out in a hurry."

"They're too close! We'd never get away from them!"

She had a point, Conrad decided. They would have a running fight on their hands. It would be better to make a stand where they had some cover.

"All right. If the train stops and there's time to get you on it, we will. Then Arturo and I can keep Leatherwood busy while the train pulls out. If you make it on board, find the conductor and tell him Conrad Browning said to make sure you get to San Francisco safely."

She stared at him for a second. "Who *are* you? Your name carries that much weight with the railroad?"

"Don't worry about it, just do what I told you."

Selena nodded. "All right. I need my saddlebags, though. Everything I own in the world is in them."

"Hurry, then," Conrad urged.

While Selena climbed down, he went to the edge of the platform and called to Arturo, "Pitch my rifle up here!"

"Are we going to make a stand?"

Conrad glanced at the train and the dust cloud. "It's starting to look like it!"

Arturo fetched Conrad's Winchester and tossed it into the air next to the platform. Conrad reached out and caught the rifle by the barrel. It wouldn't be long until the riders were in range. He wished he could see them a little better. He didn't want to start blazing away at them without being absolutely certain they were Jackson Leatherwood and the avenging angels.

He glanced down and saw Selena taking her saddlebags off her horse. She slung them over her shoulder and went to the corner of the shed where she could see the train and the approaching riders. Conrad could tell by the stiff stance of her slim body how tense she was.

The dust cloud suddenly changed direction, and veered to the east, toward Navajo Wash. For a moment Conrad couldn't figure out what they were doing. The realization burst on his brain as the riders closed in on the tracks and began shooting.

Leatherwood was making a smart move. Having figured out his quarry was at the water tank, he wanted the train to highball on through without stopping—without even slowing down—leaving Conrad, Selena, and Arturo stuck there.

It would appear Leatherwood and his companions were trying to stop the train. The engineer and fireman in the locomotive's cab would assume it was a holdup, and not stop to take on water.

Conrad bit back a curse. The range was long, but he leveled the Winchester and started firing at the horsemen. He still couldn't be completely sure they were Leatherwood and the other gunmen, but their attack on the train made it clear they weren't on the same side as Conrad and his companions. If he could force them to break off their attack, the train still might stop.

A shrill whistle came from the locomotive and it surged ahead faster, barreling along the tracks at top speed. The gunmen had accomplished their goal. They threw a few more shots at the train just to speed it along, then slowed their horses and began to fall back. They paralleled the tracks and rode steadily toward the water tank.

The train passed them, and suddenly the riders lunged their mounts across the tracks and galloped alongside the caboose where Conrad couldn't see them. Even running flat out, the horses couldn't keep up with the train for more than a few moments, but that was long enough to shield the men until the train reached the water stop and roared on past the tank.

"Get behind the shed!" Conrad shouted to Arturo and Selena, bellowing at the top of his lungs to be heard over the train's nearly deafening rumble.

Conrad retreated along the curve of the tank as the train flashed past. Smoke billowed from the locomotive's diamond-shaped stack and stung his eyes and nose, making it difficult to see and breathe. Dropping to a knee, he brought the rifle to his shoulder as he caught a glimpse of Leatherwood through a gap in the smoke. The man's ugly face was unmistakable.

Leatherwood spotted Conrad's movement and pointed the gun in his hand upward. "Up there on the tank! Kill him!"

Conrad squeezed off a shot first, but even as the Winchester blasted, Leatherwood jerked his horse aside. Smoke and flame geysered from the muzzle of his gun as he fired twice. Conrad heard the bullets thud into the tank.

He levered the rifle and sprayed slugs across the tracks as fast as he could. From down below he heard the whipcrack of more shots as Arturo joined in the fight. Conrad saw one of the avenging angels send his horse leaping across the tracks, and knew the man was trying to get behind the shed.

"Be careful of the girl!" Leatherwood roared. The gun in his hand slammed out more shots.

Water spurted from several holes in the tank where bullets had drilled through the pitch-coated wood, giving Conrad an idea as he saw the third man force his horse across the tracks next to the tank. He ran around the narrow platform to the long, spring-loaded spout, grabbed it, and jerked it down. Water shot from it, arcing across the tracks and hitting Leatherwood. Unprepared, Leather-wood choked and reeled in the saddle, and his horse began to buck.

Tossing his empty rifle to the ground, Conrad wrapped his arms around the metal spout and slid down a couple feet, then let go and dropped to the ground next to the thick beams that served as legs under the tank. He landed lightly and his Colt flickered out as he spotted the man who had just ridden across the tracks. Ten feet away, the man swung his gun toward Conrad, but Conrad fired first. His bullet ripped through the man's Adam's apple and he toppled backward out of the saddle as blood fountained from his ruined throat.

More shots came from behind the shed. Conrad worried about Arturo and Selena, but couldn't go to their aid. Throwing himself to the side he landed behind one of the thick legs as Leatherwood started shooting at him again. Conrad sent a couple of shots whistling back at the leader of the avenging angels.

A rifle cracked behind Conrad. He glanced over his shoulder and saw Arturo crouched at the corner of the shed, firing at Leatherwood. Conrad's heart leaped at the realization that Arturo must have been able to deal with the man who had ridden around the shed to attack him. His friend was all right, or at least still in the fight, and now they outnumbered Leatherwood.

The scar-faced triggerite figured that out, too. Suddenly he whirled his horse and put the spurs to it. The animal leaped into a gallop, headed to the north away from the water tank. Conrad and Arturo both fired after him, but Leatherwood never slowed down.

Leatherwood was willing to get other men killed

trying to follow Elder Hissop's orders, Conrad thought, but he wasn't devoted enough to face two-to-one odds by himself. The leader of the avenging angels was out of handgun range, so Conrad stood up and started to reload. Arturo took a couple more potshots at Leatherwood, but Conrad knew the chances of him hitting anything were small.

Arturo lowered the rifle and looked over at Conrad. "Sir, are you injured?"

"No, I'm fine. How about you?"

"I'm not—what's the word?—ventilated. But not for lack of trying on the part of that man who galloped around the shed. He hesitated when he shouldn't have, though, probably out of fear that one of his errant shots would strike Miss Webster, and I was able to drill him."

Conrad smiled. "Good for you. Did you make sure he was dead?"

Arturo's eyes widened. "Oh, my word. I should have done that, shouldn't I?"

He turned and ran behind the shed.

Conrad checked on the man he had shot, but considering what a gory mess his bullet had made of the man's throat, there wasn't much chance of him still being alive. Sure enough, the gunman was dead, and as Conrad straightened from that task, Arturo came trotting back around the shed.

"He's deceased," Arturo reported. "Next time I'll make sure of that right away." He caught his breath. "Next time? Good Lord, what am I saying? I hope there *isn't* a next time."

"I do, too," Conrad said.

But they both knew better.

Chapter 11

Conrad picked up his rifle, then started around the shed to check on Selena. He assumed she was all right, otherwise Arturo would have said something about her being hurt, but he wanted to see that with his own eyes.

She met him when he was only partway there, hurrying around the shed and unexpectedly throwing herself in his arms. Instinctively, he held her and felt the way her body trembled against his.

"So much shooting," she said in a strained voice. "I thought for sure I was going to die."

"The thought crossed my mind, too," Conrad admitted. "For all of us."

She lifted her head so she could look up at him. "What about Leatherwood?"

"He's gone. Once he was the only one left, he didn't have the stomach for a fight anymore."

"He'll be back," Selena said. "He'll get some more men, and he'll come after us. He'll never give up, and neither will Father Agony."

Conrad shook his head. "That won't matter. By

then we'll have a good lead on them and they won't be able to catch us. We can reach the Nevada line in a couple days."

"You don't think that will stop them, do you? It won't make any difference."

"Sure it will. We'll find another place you can get on the train. There'll be another westbound tomorrow or the next day."

She sighed. "You're probably right. It's just that . . . I'll believe it when I see it."

Conrad didn't blame her for being doubtful. They had been very lucky to keep her out of Leatherwood's hands so far. Sooner or later that good fortune was bound to run out.

There were two more bodies to bury, and since Leatherwood had already fled, Conrad figured there was time to do that. He got the shovel from the buggy and went behind the shed. Arturo had drilled the man, all right. He lay on his back with a single bullet wound to the chest. It was a good shot, Conrad thought.

He noticed Selena's saddlebags lying against the shed's rear wall. She'd had them draped over her shoulder when she and Arturo had retreated back there. Conrad supposed they had slipped off during the shooting, and she'd been so upset she had forgotten about them. Without really thinking about it, he bent to pick them up and put them back in the buggy before he started digging the fresh grave.

A frown creased his forehead as he straightened and felt the weight of the saddlebags. They were heavier than they would have been if Selena had filled them with food and other supplies before she left Juniper Canyon.

At that moment, she hurried around the corner of the shed, only to stop short at the sight of Conrad standing there holding the saddlebags. "What are you doing?" she asked with a slightly frantic note in her voice.

"I saw your saddlebags and thought I'd do you a favor by putting them back in the buggy." Conrad shook them up and down a little and heard faint clinking sounds from inside the pouches. "I figured they were full of provisions."

Selena came toward him and stretched out a hand. "I'll take those."

"Not just yet." Anger had begun to smolder inside Conrad. "I think I'll have a look in here first."

"You can't! You don't have any right—"

"Arturo and I have risked our lives several times for you, and as you pointed out, we haven't even known you for a full day yet." His voice was flat and hard. "I think that gives me the right to know exactly who—and what—we've been fighting for."

Selena stared at him with a mixture of anger and fear on her face. "Please . . ." she said softly.

Conrad ignored her. He unfastened the catch on

one of the bags, opened the flap, and turned it upside down.

A stream of gold and silver coins cascaded out and landed on the sandy ground with a musical tinkling as they piled up.

Selena glared at him. "Are you satisfied now?"

Conrad shook the last few coins out of the pouch, then toed them, spreading them out so he could get a good look at them. He saw five- and ten-dollar coins and an abundance of gold double eagles worth twenty dollars apiece. There had to be close to a thousand dollars lying on the ground at his feet, maybe more. Judging by the weight of the other saddlebag, it contained just as much.

"So Father Agony didn't send his avenging angels after you just because he's determined to marry you."

"You had no right to do that," Selena snapped, "and you have no right to judge me, either. You don't know what it's been like living there for the past few years, knowing that . . . that toad! . . . was determined to have me. You don't know what it's like to be sold like a piece of meat by your own father!"

Arturo came around the shed with a puzzled look on his face. "Is there some prob—Oh." His eyes widened at the sight of the pile of coins on the ground. "Oh, my."

Conrad dropped the saddlebags next to the money. "That's why you wouldn't let either of us tend to your horse. You didn't want us picking up those bags and realizing something was in them besides supplies. You were afraid we wouldn't help you if we knew you were a thief."

"I tell you, it wasn't like that!" Selena insisted. "I earned that money. I earned it in fear and loathing. I had to stand with a smile on my face while Hissop leered at me and patted me on the head and told me that someday I would be his wife. And my father stood right there smiling, too!"

"I'm sorry you had to go through that," Conrad said. "And I don't mean to judge you. Lord knows, I've done plenty of things myself that I'm not proud of. But you could have told us about this. That way we would have known Leatherwood and the others were after you because of something other than Hissop's wounded pride."

"What difference would it have made? Leatherwood still would have tried to kill you and take me back to Juniper Canyon, no matter what the reason."

Conrad had to admit she had a point. Once the lines were drawn and Leatherwood regarded him and Arturo as enemies, the violence would have played out the same way as long as the two of them tried to protect Selena. And Conrad also had to admit he wouldn't have abandoned her and allowed Leatherwood to take her back to Hissop, even if he had known about the money.

He gestured toward the coins. "Just to be

clear . . . you did steal this from Hissop, is that right?"

Selena's chin jutted out defiantly. "Yes, I did. And I'd do it again."

"You don't have any money your mother saved to help you get away?"

"No. My father always kept her on too tight a rein to allow anything like that."

"You didn't happen to kill anybody when you stole the money and ran off, did you?"

Selena stared at him in evident disbelief. "Of course not! I wouldn't do a thing like that."

Conrad nudged the pile of coins with his boot. "Maybe not, but you've already done more than I would have expected just to look at you. That's why one of those gunmen reacted like he did when I called you an innocent young woman. He said I was a fool for thinking that."

Selena shook her head. "You're not, Conrad. This is the only thing I've kept from you, and I only did it because I . . . was afraid. Think about it. You don't know me, but I don't really know you and Arturo, either. It wasn't that I was afraid you wouldn't help me. I was afraid if you knew about the money, you'd take it for yourselves and leave me for Leatherwood!"

"Miss Webster has a point, sir," Arturo put in. "For all she knew when she met us, we might have been outlaws. Utter scoundrels. Cads. Bounders."

"I get the idea, Arturo." Conrad looked at Selena. "I don't like being lied to, but I don't suppose you really did that. You just didn't tell us the whole truth. And you're right that it wouldn't have changed anything. So I guess"—he shrugged—"I guess I'm sorry. This money is your business, not ours. I'll pick it up."

"That's all right." She hurried forward and dropped to her knees next to the saddlebags and the spilled coins. "I'll get it. You have other things to do."

Arturo said, "I believe she's referring to digging more graves, sir."

"I know what she means." Conrad picked up the shovel.

Selena had started stuffing the coins back in the saddlebags. She paused and looked up at Conrad. "You're still going to take me to Nevada, or wherever you can put me on the train?"

"That's right. Leatherwood and Hissop won't get their hands on you if I can help it."

"Thank you. I swear, I won't lie to you again."

Conrad nodded. He walked several yards away, and a moment later the shovel blade bit into the sandy ground as he began to dig.

Chapter 12

By the middle of the day, the three travelers had put the water stop at Navajo Wash far behind them. They headed west, following the railroad. No more trains had come along, westbound or eastbound.

The landscape became even more arid, fully deserving of the name "desert." Occasional clumps of grass and twisted, stunted mesquite trees were the only vegetation. Those plants didn't provide much color. Everywhere Conrad looked, his eyes saw only browns, tans, grays, and now and then a splash of red sandstone. He spotted a hawk gliding along high overhead in the silver-blue sky. A lizard scuttled out of their path and into some rocks. Those were the only signs of life as the threesome made their way toward the mountains.

They had too many horses to tie them to the buggy, so Conrad hazed the animals along like a remuda on a cattle drive. Not that he had ever actually *been* on a cattle drive. His father had, though, and Frank Morgan had told him stories about those days. After the Civil War, Frank had wanted nothing more than to return to the ranch in Texas where he'd worked as a cowboy and lived a peaceful life there. Fate had intervened when a bully who fancied himself a fast gun had forced him into a fight. That was when Frank— and the rest of the world—had found out just how fast and accurate he was with a six-gun. A reputation was born, and nothing had ever been the same for Frank Morgan after that.

Conrad knew the feeling. He had been through a number of life-altering events of his own in the past few years, starting with the day his mother had introduced him to Frank and broken the news that the famous gunfighter was Conrad's real father.

Sometimes a fatalistic gloom gripped him and he believed everything had been predetermined from that moment: his marriage to Rebel, her tragic death, his transformation from a business-man into a deadly gunman who had literally killed more men than he could remember. Although he never lost any sleep over the lives he had ended —he never shot to kill except in self-defense or to save the life of someone else—it seemed like he ought to at least be able to recall the men he had killed. Their deaths tended to blend into a haze of powdersmoke and blood.

"Conrad, what's wrong?" Selena asked from the buggy seat. "You look like your thoughts are a million miles away."

He shook his head and smiled. "Not that far. I'm fine." He glanced at the sky, where the sun was almost directly overhead and beating down with a fierce heat. "We need to find some shade and stop for a while to let the horses rest and cool off."

"I'm not sure where you're going to find any shade out here," Arturo said. "The last place I saw land this flat and empty was down in New Mexico."

"The *Jornada del Muerto*," Conrad said, recalling how he and Arturo had first met, back when Arturo still worked for one of Conrad's enemies. Or rather, for one of Kid Morgan's enemies, since at that time Conrad had considered his past life dead and buried. "Yes, this is almost as bad. Maybe we can find another trestle and stop under it for a while, or some rocks big enough to give us some shade."

That hope appeared to be an empty one. Even though they stopped from time to time to rest the horses, the heat drained man and beast alike of their energy. Arturo and Selena had it better because at least they had the meager shade provided by the buggy's canopy, but the sun was getting to them, too.

Arturo said, "I've never understood how it can be so hot during the day in this region and yet so cold at night."

"That's the way the desert is," Conrad said. "I think it must have something to do with how dry the air is. There's nothing to hold in the heat."

"You're probably right. That doesn't, however, make me feel any better."

It didn't make any of them feel better. Another hour crept by. Weariness gripped Conrad and made him sway in the saddle. He fought to stay awake.

Suddenly he spotted something ahead of them and lifted his head. He raised himself in the stirrups to get a better look. A narrow pinnacle of rock jutted into the air. He pointed at it. "Look there."

Selena said, "That must be what they call Finger Rock. I've heard of it, but I've never been here."

"They could call it Thumb Rock or Toe Rock as far as I'm concerned," Arturo said. "As long as it provides some shade, I'm glad to see it."

With renewed energy, they kept moving toward the promised shelter. For every yard they covered, Finger Rock seemed to recede an equal distance, but gradually the gap narrowed. They reached it in mid-afternoon. The rock was twenty feet wide at its base, tapering to a much narrower point sixty feet in the air. The shade it cast on its eastern side was welcome, and the air felt almost blessedly cool.

Conrad unsaddled all the horses, including Selena's. Her saddlebags were in the back of the buggy now that there was no longer any need to keep their contents secret. Conrad didn't think any of the horses would stray very far from the shade, so he hobbled them but didn't picket them.

"We'll stay here until after dark. That'll give us

a chance to rest and cool off. We can probably travel most of the night. It won't be hard to follow the railroad, even in the dark."

"What about Leatherwood?" Selena asked. "How long would it take him to get back to Juniper Canyon from Navajo Wash?"

"At least half a day, I suppose."

"And once he got there he'd have to round up more men and fresh horses," Conrad said. "That would take a while. So at the very best, he couldn't have started after us again until a little while ago. If anything happened to delay him, he might not be on the trail yet. We'll be able to stay ahead of him. Anyway, we had to stop and rest the horses. Pretty soon they wouldn't have been able to go on, and then we really would've been stuck."

"I suppose you're right. I'll just be glad when I know I'm somewhere he can't get at me any-more."

Conrad didn't say it, but he knew that wasn't really possible. They could make it very difficult for Leatherwood to find Selena, practically impossible, in fact, but the chance that he might track her down would always exist. A man who devoted all his time and energy, even his very life, to something was hard to stop. The question was whether or not Jackson Leatherwood was that stubborn.

Selena sat down with her back propped against the rock pinnacle, and within a few minutes she was asleep. Conrad and Arturo were giving water to the horses when Conrad said, "You might as well get some shut-eye, too."

"What about you?" Arturo asked. "Neither of us has gotten much sleep in the past twenty-four hours."

"That's true, but I'll be all right. You doze for a while, then I'll wake you."

"Very well." Arturo took a blanket from the buggy and spread it on the ground to sit on. He folded another blanket and stuck it behind his head to use as a pillow when he leaned back against the rock. Tipping his derby down over his face, he folded his arms across his chest, and soon dozed off.

Conrad hunkered on his heels and sipped from one of the canteens. He didn't drink much. He didn't know when they would find more.

He was still a little irritated Selena had hidden that money from him. On the other hand, he understood why she had done it. He couldn't blame her for not completely trusting him and Arturo. Growing up in a Mormon community, she might have been taught all Gentiles were not trustworthy. Conrad didn't know much about what they believed. Like most people, he was aware Mormon men sometimes had multiple wives, but that was about the extent of his knowledge.

He struggled to stay awake for a couple hours

while Arturo and Selena slept. Then, quietly so as not to disturb Selena, he shook Arturo awake and took his place. In two more hours, the sun would be down and they could think about moving on.

Sleep came down on Conrad like a sledge-hammer. When he woke up, his face was beaded with sweat and he didn't know how long he had been lost in deep, dreamless slumber.

All he knew was that somebody had just screamed.

Chapter 13

Conrad bolted up from the ground. His gun was in his hand without him even thinking about it. The sun was down but a faint rosy glow remained in the sky. When Selena screamed again and Conrad swung toward her, the light was bright enough for him to see the large scorpion that had climbed onto her arm and was now crawling over her shoulder toward the open throat of her shirt. If the venomous creature got inside the shirt, it was bound to sting her. Conrad knew the sting of a scorpion that large might sicken Selena for days and really slow their flight from Leatherwood.

He sprang toward her, reaching out with the Colt. Moving with the same speed that made him such a deadly gunman, he used the revolver's barrel to flick the scorpion away. It landed on the ground near Arturo, who brought his boot heel down on it with crushing force before the scorpion could scuttle away.

Selena stopped screaming, but still shuddered as she looked down at her shoulder where the scorpion had been. Conrad holstered his gun and held out a hand to her.

"Come on. Better get up in case any more of the critters are stirring around here."

That got Selena's attention. She grasped his hand and let him pull her to her feet. She turned around in front of him. "Are there any more of them on me?"

"I don't see any." Conrad was slightly amused even though he knew the situation could have been serious.

Selena noticed him smiling and punched his shoulder. "Stop that! Don't laugh at me. That awful thing could have stung me."

"I know. That's why I knocked it away. You're welcome."

"Oh." She looked contrite. "I'm sorry, Conrad. Of course, I meant to thank you. I just . . . when I opened my eyes and saw that thing . . . I was so scared."

"It's fine," he assured her.

"Were you asleep?"

"I was, but it was time for me to wake up anyway." He gestured at the fading light in the sky. "We'll eat a little, give the horses some water, then get moving again."

By the time they were ready to go, the last of the light from the sun was gone. The glow of a million stars had replaced it. The heat of the day disappeared as the cool night breeze sprung up.

Conrad drove the extra horses along the railroad right-of-way while Arturo and Selena followed in the buggy. The miles fell behind them quickly.

After several hours, low, dark humps appeared in front of them. Hills, Conrad realized. Several small mountain ranges stretched across the isolated country along the Utah-Nevada border. After the flat, arid desert, the higher country would be a relief. On the other side of the border, the terrain dropped again to the vast Humboldt Basin, which was as bad or worse than the country in Utah, but at least there were a few small towns along the rail line. They would be able to put Selena on a train bound for San Francisco. As Conrad had mused earlier, once Selena reached the city by the bay, she wouldn't be completely out of Leatherwood's reach, but at least he would have a lot harder time finding her. Conrad planned to send a wire to his lawyers, Claudius Turnbuckle and John J. Stafford, asking them to help Selena. He was sure they would find a safe place for her.

"I've never been this far away from home," Selena said in wonder. "In fact, there were times I asked myself if there really was a world outside Juniper Canyon. The elders like to teach that the world beyond the bounds of our home is nothing but a wasteland."

"That's a good way to keep the young people from getting restless and wanting to leave, I suppose," Conrad said.

"I'm sure that's part of it, but the way my people have been persecuted, I'm sure sometimes it does seem like the rest of the world is a savage, terrible place."

From everything Conrad had heard, the Mormons had indeed suffered from persecution in the past, but they had done their own share of persecuting, too, including more than one massacre of Gentiles who didn't share their beliefs. He had no interest in arguing religion with Selena or anybody else, so he didn't say anything, just kept pushing the little horse herd westward.

The heavens were gray with dawn in the east and the moon was a glimmering crescent hanging in the western sky when they stopped again. For the past hour they had been following the railroad through rugged, humpbacked hills. When they came to a dry wash that cut through those hills, Conrad called a halt.

"I don't want to try to get the buggy through that wash until we can see better. Those banks can be tricky. We don't want to bust a wheel or an axle. Besides, the horses can use some rest again."

"So can I," Selena said.

Conrad and Arturo picketed the horses to make sure the animals didn't stray. While they were tending to that chore, Conrad suddenly smelled smoke and turned to see that Selena had gathered some broken greasewood branches and kindled a fire. The flames leaped brightly.

"What are you doing?" he asked as he strode over to the fire. The sharp tone of his voice made Selena look up in surprise.

"Why, I thought you and Arturo might like some coffee this morning," she said. "Besides, it's a little chilly again."

"Yes, but you didn't even try to hide that fire." Conrad started kicking dirt on the flames, causing Selena to gasp and move back hurriedly.

"What are you doing?"

"Putting it out so Leatherwood won't be able to follow it right to us." Conrad glanced off toward the flats east of them. "That is, if he hasn't already seen it."

"But I thought you said he'd be a long way behind us."

"You can see these hills for a long way out there," Conrad told her. "If Leatherwood pushed his men hard during the day yesterday and rode on through the night, he could be close enough behind us to have spotted that fire."

"Oh, my God," Selena breathed. "I'm sorry, Conrad. I didn't even think of that. I . . . I just wanted to do something nice for the two of you."

"Chances are he didn't see it. The fire was pretty small, and it didn't burn for very long. But there's no point in running that risk when we don't have to. I'll build a fire pit from some rocks. That way we can have coffee and some hot food without giving away where we are."

"You're right. Of course you're right. From now on I won't do anything like that without asking you about it first."

Conrad went back to the horses, and when he was finished with them he built that fire pit, stacking up rocks in a ring until he could start a blaze inside it without the flames being seen. Arturo took over from there, boiling coffee and frying some hotcakes and bacon. After the hectic, dangerous day-and-a-half they'd had, it felt mighty good to sit and eat and wash the food down with hot coffee.

"Before the day is over, we'll be in Nevada," Conrad said. "Might even find a town by then and get you on the train. There should be a westbound along sometime today."

"I can't thank you and Arturo enough for everything you've done," Selena said. "If not for the two of you, Leatherwood and his men would have taken me back to—"

Conrad held up a hand to stop her. He lifted his head and listened intently. He had heard something out of place, like the stealthy scrape of boot leather on rocky ground. He dropped his plate and started to his feet. His hand streaked to his gun. As the Colt came out of the holster, men appeared in the gray dawn light, surrounding the camp and leveling rifles at him and Arturo.

"Don't move!" a voice rasped. "Drop that gun, mister."

"Please, Conrad," Selena said, sending a shock through him as she went on, "Do what he tells you."

The man who had given the order chuckled. "Yeah, you better listen to my wife, mister."

Slowly, Conrad turned his head to look over his shoulder at Selena. She had drawn a small pistol from under that loose man's shirt she wore, and had the gun pointed at him.

"Well, hell," Conrad said.

Chapter 14

"Starting that fire wasn't just a thoughtless accident," Conrad went on. "It was a signal."

The gun in Selena's hand didn't waver as she came to her feet. "That's right. I'm sorry, Conrad—"

"Save your apologies," he said.

From the other side of the fire, Arturo said, "I'm confused. I thought you were supposed to marry Elder Agonistes Hissop, Miss Webster."

The man laughed again. "She can't marry anybody. She's already married to me. Maybe not as far as Father Agony or the rest of his followers are concerned, but we had our own ceremony and it's good enough for me."

"I'll handle this, Daniel," Selena said as she circled the fire, keeping the pistol in her hand trained on Conrad. She told him, "I'd really feel better if you dropped that gun."

Conrad had done a quick head count of the men who had snuck up on the camp. There were eight of them. He had gone up against four-to-one odds before and lived through those fights, but it wasn't really four to one because Arturo couldn't account for as many men as Conrad could. A gun battle would get them both killed, and despite Selena's betrayal, he didn't want to endanger her life from any stray bullets.

With that thought in mind, he bent slowly and placed his Colt on the ground. Then he straightened and stepped back away from it.

"That's good," the man called Daniel said with an approving nod. He motioned with his rifle and told Arturo, "Get over there with your friend, mister, and leave your Winchester where it is."

Arturo stood up and joined Conrad. "Are you going to kill us?" he asked Daniel, sounding interested, but not particularly concerned.

Without hesitation, Selena answered, "Of course not. The two of you helped me. I owe you my life." She looked over at the man. "Do you hear me, Daniel? I don't want them hurt."

"That'll be up to them," Daniel said.

In the growing light, Conrad could see he was a little older than Selena, probably in his early twenties. Slender and medium height, he had dark hair and a wisp of dark beard. His companions, all roughly the same age, wore range clothes and battered hats. They all carried Winchesters or Henry rifles, and several of them had holstered revolvers on their hips. Judging by their faces, they weren't true hardcases, but they all had the stamp of hard living on them. It showed up in gaunt, hollow cheeks and haunted eyes.

"You'll cooperate, won't you, Conrad?" Selena asked.

"I don't much like being played for a fool," he answered, "but Arturo and I aren't interested in causing trouble for you. You ought to know that by now. Just take your horse and go with your friends. We'll go on about our business."

Selena turned to Daniel. "That's fair enough, isn't it?" Despite what she had said to him about her doing the handling, it was obvious she was going to defer to whatever decisions he made.

"I don't know," Daniel said. "*I* don't much like the way you call him Conrad, like the two of you are old friends or something."

"They *are* my friends. Didn't you hear me?

Conrad and Arturo saved my life more than once. If not for them, Jackson Leatherwood and the rest of Father Agony's avenging angels would have caught me and taken me back to Juniper Canyon."

"Well, then, I guess I should be thanking them," Daniel said. "Why don't you introduce us properly?"

"All right. This is Conrad Browning and Arturo Vincenzo."

Conrad's name obviously didn't mean anything to the young man. He looked at Arturo and said, "Vincenzo . . . That's an Italian name, isn't it? What's an Italian doing out here in Utah, especially one who sounds more like an Englishman?"

"I prefer to think of myself as a citizen of the world," Arturo replied. "But to answer your implied question about my accent, I was educated in England and spent a considerable amount of time there, as well as in my native Italy and in this country. As a matter of fact, I speak five languages fluently and have more than a smattering of several others."

"Oh," Daniel said with a mocking grin. "Smart man."

"Evidently not, or I wouldn't find myself stuck in this wilderness surrounded by people who keep trying to kill me."

"Nobody's killing anybody," Selena said. "The killing is over and done with. Right, Daniel?"

He shrugged. "Sure, whatever you say, Selena. I just want you to be happy."

Conrad wasn't sure Daniel meant that. In fact, he felt an instinctive dislike and distrust of the young man.

"You told your friend who we are," Conrad said, "but you didn't introduce him and these other fellas to us."

"Well, we sure don't want to be impolite," Daniel said, still wearing a smug grin. "My name's Daniel Kingman. Me and the rest of these boys . . . we call ourselves the Outcast Saints."

"Daniel and the others . . . were forced to leave Juniper Canyon," Selena said. She had lowered her gun, but Kingman and the others still had their rifles pointed at Conrad and Arturo. "They voiced opposition to some of Elder Hissop's decisions, so he accused them of being blasphemers."

"Yes, but the main reason Father Agony wanted to get rid of us is because we're young. We didn't want to wait around while he and the rest of the older men took all the girls as their wives. And they sure as hell didn't want the girls deciding they'd like to have younger men for husbands."

It all sounded foreign to Conrad, almost incomprehensible that people could live like that. They had a right to their own religious beliefs, of course, but to drive out their own young men . . . well, it just didn't make sense.

From what he'd heard about Elder Agonistes Hissop, he wasn't too surprised the man wanted to get rid of anyone who disagreed with him or represented a threat to his plans.

Selena said, "After Daniel and the others were banished, I decided I had to leave Juniper Canyon, too. I just had to wait until the time was right."

"Until you could get your hands on Father Agony's treasure," Kingman said. "Did you get it, Selena?"

She frowned at him, as if she was surprised at the eagerness and greed evident in his voice. "I got it, but it's not really what I would call a treasure, Daniel. It's two thousand dollars, maybe a little more."

"When you're broke and hungry, two thousand dollars sounds like a treasure to me! Where is it? I want to see it."

Selena pushed her hair back. "In my saddlebags, behind the seat in the buggy."

Kingman turned to one of the other men. "Fetch them, Ollie."

The man called Ollie, who was big and had a shock of blond hair under a pushed-back hat, went to the buggy and came back with the saddlebags dangling from a hamlike fist. He held them out. "Here they are, Dan."

Kingman tucked his rifle under his arm and snatched the saddlebags from Ollie. He opened one of the pouches and plunged his hand inside. When he brought it out, coins flowed through his fingers and jingled as they fell back into the leather bag. A grin stretched across his lean face. "Beautiful," he muttered.

Conrad thought there was something seriously wrong with a man who could call a bunch of coins beautiful when he had a woman like Selena Webster standing next to him, but to each his own, he supposed.

The men had relaxed a little, and the feeling of impending violence wasn't as thick in the air. Conrad said, "All right, you've got the girl and the money. You've got what you wanted. Why don't you let Arturo and me get our guns, and we'll be on our way. You can even take those extra horses with you."

Kingman closed and fastened the saddlebags and tossed them back to Ollie. "Oh, we'll take the horses, all right. And the buggy." He made a curt gesture, and the rest of the Outcast Saints lifted their rifles again. "And you two, as well," Kingman went on. "You're either coming with us . . . or we'll bury you right here."

Chapter 15

"Daniel, no!" Selena cried. "There's no reason to do that. They helped me. They can't do anything to hurt us."

"Oh, no?" Kingman asked. "What if Leatherwood catches up to them, and they tell him you're with me? What if they tell him which way we went?"

"Leatherwood tried to kill them twice. They don't have any reason to cooperate with him!"

"Not even to get back at you for lying to them? Or to save themselves from being tortured? Because you know Leatherwood is perfectly capable of that if he gets his hands on them." Kingman jerked a hand toward Conrad and Arturo. "Anyway, how do you know what these two might do? You barely know them!"

"I know they saved my life," Selena told him in a half whisper.

"And I appreciate that." Kingman turned to his men. "Get their guns. Tie their hands and put them on horses. We need to get out of here. We've already wasted too much time. I can feel Leatherwood out there."

So could Conrad, and he wasn't sure who was the bigger threat: the fanatical avenging angel or the bitter young outcast.

In a quiet voice, Arturo asked, "Sir, how are we going to respond to this provocation?"

"Play along with them for now," Conrad answered. "This isn't our fight, and maybe after a while they'll realize we don't want any part of it."

Kingman sent a couple men back along the wash for the group's horses, which they had hidden while they were sneaking up on the camp after spotting Selena's signal fire. While that was going on, the other Outcast Saints gathered up Conrad's and Arturo's guns, then tied their wrists together in front of them. That was better than having their hands tied behind their backs, Conrad supposed. It was more comfortable, anyway.

Even though he didn't like Kingman, he didn't want to fight with the man or with the other young Mormons who had been driven away from their homes. He thought about his lost children, still hidden somewhere as part of Pamela's twisted revenge on him, and wished briefly he and Arturo had never gotten mixed up in Selena's troubles.

But that was a wasted wish, Conrad thought. He knew he couldn't have ridden off and left her in danger, no matter what sort of person she had turned out to be. Rebel's disapproval would have haunted him forever if he'd done that.

The sun was up, flooding the hills with golden light. A couple men hitched the team to the buggy and led the animals across the railroad tracks. The wheels of the empty buggy bumped over the rails. Once the vehicle was north of the tracks, one of the men climbed into it to handle the reins.

The others lifted Conrad and Arturo into saddles. "I'm not the best rider in the world," Arturo warned, "but I'll do my best to keep up."

"You'd better," Kingman warned. "You won't like it if we have to leave you behind."

"I really wish you'd stop threatening them," Selena said.

"Of course." Once again, Kingman sounded like he didn't mean it.

Everyone mounted up and rode northward through the hills. The young man called Ollie led the way. Conrad and Arturo were in the middle of the group, with their captors bunched around them so they couldn't get away. Conrad didn't intend to try. He still hoped he could get Kingman to listen to reason. Even if he wasn't able to do that, maybe Selena could.

She dropped back beside him and said quietly, "I'm sorry about this, Conrad, I truly am. I never intended for you and Arturo to get hurt. When I escaped from Juniper Canyon, I didn't have any idea I would run into you."

"Just out of curiosity, what was your plan?" he asked. "Were you supposed to rendezvous with your friends here in these hills?"

"That's right. I was going to follow the railroad until I reached the hills, and Daniel and his friends would be waiting and watching for my signal fire. I hoped I would be a lot farther away from the canyon before anyone discovered I was gone. Somehow, Elder Hissop found out almost right away and sent Leatherwood and the others after me. That almost ruined everything. It would have . . . if not for you."

"Too bad that doesn't seem to mean anything to Kingman. He's not happy about you being back here talking to me."

Conrad had seen the young man cast several suspicious glances over his shoulder since Selena had dropped back instead of riding beside him. The glare Kingman sent his way was dark and menacing.

"I don't care," Selena insisted. "Daniel can't tell me who I can talk to, or who my friends are."

Her defiance, her determination to be in charge of her own life, reminded Conrad of someone, and he didn't have to think very hard to know who it was: Rebel. She had been the same way. When he'd first met her, she had been the same sort of hard-riding, pistol-packing hellion her brothers were, and she hadn't really changed much in the years they were together. Love had softened her a little . . . but that was all.

Of course, Rebel hadn't been a thief, like Selena. It wasn't Conrad's place to judge her for stealing the money from Hissop, but she had to have known the elder would send men after her to recover it, as well as to bring her back. He might have gotten over the loss of a potential wife, but not the money.

"I won't let him hurt you." Selena went on, referring to Daniel Kingman. "He's really a good man, Conrad. You just don't know him. All the Outcast Saints are fine young men. They weren't treated fairly by Father Agony and the older men in the community."

"Life has a habit of being unfair to folks."

She didn't have any response to that.

The air quickly warmed as the sun rose in the sky, but it wasn't as blazingly hot as it had been out on the desert. By midday, the riders had left the railroad far behind and were climbing into a range of rugged, snow-capped mountains.

"These are the Prophet Mountains," Kingman said during one of the stops they made to rest the horses. "The name's appropriate, don't you think? But there's no place here for Joseph Smith or Brigham Young or even Father Agony. We're all our own prophets, and no man is going to lord it over another."

Kingman might say that, Conrad thought, but he was quick to give orders to the other men and there was no doubt who was in charge. There was an old saying about the corrupting nature of power. Conrad had a hunch he was seeing living proof of it in Daniel Kingman.

The group pushed on, and by the middle of the afternoon horses and riders were climbing a zigzag path that rose to a pass between two peaks. The mountains weren't terribly tall, but they were rugged enough that the pass appeared to be the only way through them. Selena brought her horse alongside Conrad's again and turned in the saddle to point to the right across an expanse of arid, blindingly white flats that stretched for miles before they ended in another range of mountains.

"Juniper Canyon is in those mountains on the other side of the flats," she explained.

Conrad frowned. "They're what, twenty miles away?"

"That's right." Selena nodded. "We've come the long way around and made a big circle. It would never occur to Father Agony that Daniel and the others are right here, just across the salt flats, because nobody crosses that stretch. The flats are too dry and too dangerous."

Arturo said, "Conrad and I traveled through a terrible desert down in New Mexico called the *Jornada del Muerto*. We told you about that. The name means 'Journey of the Dead Man,' although some people take it to mean simply 'the Journey of Death,' which is a good name for it. It's very dry and much more extensive than those flats appear to be. It can take days to make the journey."

"The crust of salt on the flats can crack under too much weight, and when it does it cuts a horse's hooves so badly the horse can't walk.

That's why no one tries to cross it. They would probably wind up on foot and stranded."

"I see. There's dried lava much like that in the *Jornada del Muerto*—"

"It's not a competition," Conrad broke in with a note of frustration in his voice. "Both places are pretty bad. We can probably leave it at that."

They reached the pass and rode through it. Conrad hadn't been impressed by much of anything he had seen in Utah, but as the pass opened up into a valley that fell away on the far side of the mountains, he was surprised. Instead of the ugly browns and tans that met the eye everywhere else the valley below him was painted with the verdant green of grass and trees and decorated with splashes of color from wildflowers.

Kingman and Selena had reined in, and Conrad, Arturo, and the other men followed suit. Kingman turned in his saddle to smirk at the prisoners.

"Welcome to the Valley of the Outcast Saints."

Chapter 16

Conrad gave in to his curiosity and asked, "Where does the water come from? There has to be a better source of water than usual around here to account for all this vegetation."

"That's right," Kingman replied with a nod. "There are several springs on this side of the pass. The streams they form run through the valley. I've been exploring the place for months, ever since we came here, and I'm not sure I've even found all of them yet. The ones I have found look like someone did some blasting around them in the past to enlarge the openings and increase the flow of water. Miners, maybe, or somebody who wanted to start a ranch here. I've been tempted to try to improve them even more."

"But you're afraid the explosions might block off the springs instead," Conrad said. "You'd need to be sure the bore holes are placed correctly."

Kingman looked at him with new interest. "You know something about blasting?"

Conrad shrugged. Not only had he taken engineering courses in college, he had quite a bit of practical experience from being around the mines and the railroad lines his companies owned. Back in his old life, he had spent a considerable amount of time discussing various problems with the engineers who were working for him on those projects.

He wasn't going to tell Kingman that. He had a hunch the self-styled Outcast Saints were only one step above being outlaws. If they found out he was rich, they might decide to hold him for ransom, or something equally annoying and dangerous.

"Maybe we'll talk about it while you're here," Kingman went on. He didn't sound quite as hostile, as if talking about exploring the valley and the plans he had for it made him forget to be as arrogant as he'd been earlier.

That didn't last long, though. The cocky grin reappeared on his face as he said, "Might as well get some use out of you since we'll be feeding you." He waved the group forward. "Come on!"

With Selena trotting her horse alongside his, Kingman led the way down a trail that turned into a road running through the center of the valley. Conrad saw plowed fields with crops growing in them. He spotted fruit trees bearing colorful fruit. Water made all the difference, turning the little corner of wilderness into something of an oasis. It was hard to believe only a few miles away over the pass lay a hellish, barren, blazing desert.

Several buildings appeared up ahead. Some were log cabins, others were squarish adobe huts. Conrad saw corrals and barns. The Outcast Saints appeared to be making new lives for themselves in the valley.

And they weren't alone. Conrad spotted a couple women moving around the cabins. Selena wouldn't be the only female. He wondered if those women had run away from Juniper Canyon, too. If that was the case, it wasn't surprising Elder Hissop was getting upset. He had to be worried about losing so many marriageable women from his community. One thing you needed in a society where men took multiple wives was plenty of women, Conrad thought wryly.

Kingman took them to the largest of the log cabins. As he reined in, he turned to Selena. "This is our new home. I built it especially for you."

"It's fine, Daniel," she told him. "Really fine. I'm sure we'll be happy here." She paused. "But you could make an even better start in our new life by letting my friends go."

"In due time," Kingman said in an off-handed manner.

Conrad knew better. He had a hunch Kingman would never let him and Arturo go now that they knew the location of the Valley of the Outcast Saints. He would be too afraid they'd expose the place to Hissop and Leatherwood.

Whether Selena realized it or not, her "husband" didn't intend to allow the prisoners to ever leave the valley . . . at least not alive.

Kingman turned to Ollie. "Take several men and put these two in the smokehouse."

"Wait a minute," Selena protested. "You're going to lock them up?"

"Just until we can be certain they're trustworthy," Kingman told her. "It's for their own protection, as well. Some of the people here might not be inclined to be as tolerant of Gentiles as you are. They remember the things that have been done to believers in the past."

"Well . . . I suppose you might be right about that." Selena turned to Conrad and Arturo. "I'm sorry about this. I'm sure it won't be for long."

Conrad suspected she was right about that. A few nights from now, or maybe even tonight, Kingman would have the prisoners taken out and killed, and their bodies disposed of so no one would ever find them. Then he could tell Selena he had decided to let them go. She might wonder why Conrad and Arturo hadn't said good-bye to her before they left, but eventually she would convince herself it was better that way.

The alternative would be too upsetting for her to consider.

Kingman dismounted and stood next to Selena's horse, holding a hand up to her. "Come on," he said with a smile. "Let me show you your new home."

She smiled at him and swung down from her saddle to take his hand. Together they went into the log cabin.

Ollie moved his horse up behind Conrad and Arturo. In a firm but not unkind voice he said, "Let's go, fellas. The smokehouse won't be that comfortable, but you'll see it ain't too bad."

Three more members of the group moved their mounts up so Conrad and Arturo were surrounded again. They had no choice but to heel their horses into motion. Ollie rode around them and led the way to another log building a couple hundred yards from the cabin where Selena and Kingman had disappeared. The building had no windows, no way in or out except a thick door with a bar across it. The people of the valley might have built it as a place to smoke meat, but obviously they'd had in mind it would make a sturdy prison, too.

Conrad glanced over at Arturo and saw his friend and servant watching him. From the corner of his mouth, Conrad whispered, "We can't let them lock us up."

Arturo gave a tiny nod to show that he understood. He had figured out Kingman intended to have them killed. He had run across a number of evil men in recent years, including his own former employer.

The odds were a little better. Some of the Outcast Saints had scattered to their homes when they arrived in the valley, leaving only Ollie and three men guarding the prisoners. Conrad thought if he could get his hands on Ollie's revolver, he could deal with the other men in a hurry. He didn't particularly want to kill them, but knew sooner or later—probably sooner—their zealotry would lead them to murder him and Arturo.

Of course, even if they got away from their guardians, they would still be in the middle of the enemy stronghold. They would have to fight their way out. Conrad knew it was better to fight than to go meekly to their deaths. He managed to untie his hands—the bonds weren't that tight.

"Here we are," Ollie said as he drew rein in front of the smokehouse. He turned in the saddle and moved his hand toward the butt of his gun. "If you fellas will just get off first—"

Instead of dismounting, Conrad suddenly dug his heels into his horse's flanks and sent the animal lunging forward. Ollie let out a yell of alarm and clawed at his revolver as Conrad's horse came right at him.

Conrad kicked his feet free of the stirrups and left the saddle in a diving tackle that sent him crashing into Ollie. The unexpected impact drove Ollie backward out of his saddle. He crashed to the ground with Conrad on top of him. Conrad's left hand locked around the wrist of Ollie's gunhand, and his bunched right fist slammed down into the man's broad face. Snatching Ollie's gun from its holster, Conrad rolled away from him and came up on one knee with the revolver leveled and ready to fire.

Chapter 17

Conrad had been too busy with Ollie to know what Arturo was doing. His heart sank as he saw his friend lying facedown on the ground with one of the Outcast Saints on top of him. The man's knee dug into Arturo's back with painful force, and a gun barrel was pressed against the back of Arturo's head.

In addition, the other two men had whipped out their guns and pointed them at Conrad. He knew he was only a whisker away from being fired on. If they did, he was confident he would get lead in them, but he wouldn't make it out of there alive and neither would Arturo.

"Drop it!" the man who knelt on Arturo yelled. "Right now!"

"Better do what he says, mister," Ollie advised from where he lay on the ground a few feet away. The fall had knocked his hat off and left his shock of blond hair riffling in the breeze blowing through the valley. "If you don't, he'll blow your friend's brains out."

Back up the road, the door of Kingman's cabin flew open and the young man rushed out. If Kingman had the chance, he would order his men to shoot, and be done with the problem.

Before that could happen, Conrad lowered Ollie's Colt and put it on the ground in front of him. "Take it easy," he said as he lifted both hands into the air. "Let off on that trigger, will you?"

From his awkward, uncomfortable position, Arturo said, "I'm sorry . . . sir . . . I tried to . . . grapple with one of these men . . . and get his gun . . . but I'm not strong enough . . . or fast enough."

Conrad managed to smile. "Don't worry about it, Arturo. We did what we could."

Kingman ran up and yelled, "What's going on here? Can't you handle a simple job like locking these two up, Ollie?"

Behind him, Selena had stepped out of the cabin, too. Conrad saw her gaze worriedly toward the smokehouse. She raised a clenched hand and pressed it to the front of her shirt.

Ollie climbed to his feet and brushed himself off. "I'm sorry, Dan," he said with a contrite look on his face. "This fella Browning, well, he moves just about as fast as anybody I've ever seen. When he jumped me it was like a rattlesnake strikin'." Ollie picked up his gun and slipped it back into its holster.

"I don't care how fast he is, you shouldn't have let him get close enough to jump you." Kingman jerked a hand toward Arturo. "Get that one on his feet." He turned to Conrad, who had stood up while the other guards covered him. "If you wanted to convince me to trust you, Browning, this was the wrong way to go about it."

"We both know what you've got in mind, Kingman," Conrad said. "Trust doesn't enter into it. You just want *her* to think that."

Kingman paled at that. He turned to Ollie and barked, "Lock them up like I told you. Think you can manage that?"

"Sure, Dan." Ollie lifted the bar from the brackets

attached to the smokehouse wall on either side of the door. He leaned the bar against the wall and swung the door out. "Get in there, you two."

The man holding the gun to Arturo's head dragged him to his feet and prodded him forward. Conrad went in first. Arturo stumbled through the door behind him. With a heavy thump, the door slammed closed, plunging them into thick dark-ness. Conrad heard the scraping sound as Ollie replaced the bar in its brackets.

There were some tiny chinks here and there in the mud that plastered the logs together. Those gaps let in a few shafts of light that served to relieve the stygian gloom slightly. As Conrad's eyes adjusted to the darkness he saw the racks where sides of beef hung while they were being cured by the smoke from a fire in the pit in the center of the floor. Those racks were empty at the moment, and only cold ashes were in the fire pit.

The only unlucky creatures in the smokehouse were himself and Arturo.

"Clearly, attempting to assist Miss Webster was an unfortunate and unwise decision on our part."

"It was my fault," Conrad said. "You just went along."

"Well, of course. As your employee, it's my job to follow your orders."

"I thought we'd established that you and I are friends, too . . . and a friend can tell another friend that he's about to do a damn fool thing."

"Yes, but don't you see that you had no choice in the matter?"

Conrad frowned in the darkness. "How do you figure that?"

"You forget, sir, that I've stood guard many times while you slept. I've heard the results of the dreams that occur to you in your slumber."

"You mean I talk in my sleep?" Conrad asked in surprise.

"Well . . . not in any real coherent fashion. But I've been able to make out enough words and phrases to know that your late wife's death still haunts you. It's really no surprise when you're faced with a dilemma, you want to choose whatever course you believe she would have had you choose." Arturo paused. "I hope I'm not speaking out of turn here by saying these things, sir. As you yourself just brought up, we *are* friends."

Smiling, Conrad reached out in the darkness and found Arturo's shoulder. He squeezed it briefly. "You're not speaking out of turn at all, amigo." He took a deep breath. "Now it's time for us to start thinking about how we're going to get out of here."

Over the next few hours, Conrad inspected every inch of the smokehouse using his hands and what little he could see. He even climbed up on the drying racks, balancing precariously while he poked at the roof. He was looking for a weak

116

spot, anywhere he might make a little hole, then enlarge it into an opening big enough for him and Arturo to escape. He knew that was a real long shot, but it was better than sitting there doing nothing.

While Conrad carried out that search, Arturo investigated the possibility of digging out underneath one of the walls.

Conrad considered that pretty unlikely, but what he was doing was probably going to be futile, too. He didn't discourage Arturo.

Time passed, and finally Conrad had to say, "I can't find any place where we might be able to get out."

"Nor can I," Arturo said. "It appears that when the Outcast Saints built this structure, they dug down and sunk the first logs several inches in the ground. And the dirt is packed so hard, I'm not sure we could dig out even if we had a shovel, let alone with our bare fingers or a pocket knife. Given months, we might burrow a tunnel like moles . . . but we don't have months, do we?"

"Not likely. It wouldn't surprise me if Kingman decided to get rid of us tonight."

"Won't our abrupt departure make Miss Webster suspicious?"

"I'm sure it will. But what can she do?"

"Yes, she's cast her lot with young Mr. Kingman," Arturo said philosophically. "She can't very well admit, even to herself, that he may be as ruthless as that oddly-named religious leader from whom she escaped."

Conrad thought about Elder Hissop and also about the leader of the avenging angels, Jackson Leatherwood. He was convinced Leatherwood had gathered more men and set out once again from Juniper Canyon to search for Selena. What were the chances Leatherwood might find the valley before Kingman had Conrad and Arturo killed?

Would they be any better off if Leatherwood showed up and wiped out the Outcast Saints? Not hardly, Conrad thought. Leatherwood had a grudge against him and Arturo, too—a blood debt to settle for the men they had killed.

There was no getting around it—they didn't have a friend anywhere in that corner of Utah. The only person the least bit sympathetic to them—Selena—was powerless to aid them.

Suddenly Conrad heard footsteps approaching the smokehouse. Light still filtered through the tiny cracks in the walls, so he didn't think Kingman had sent his men to kill them just yet. He would wait until after dark for that.

But someone was definitely about to open the door, because the bar scraped out of its brackets. Conrad touched Arturo's arm. "Be ready for anything."

As the door swung open and let in a rectangle of light blinding the two men who had been shut up in darkness for hours, Conrad wasn't prepared for what Ollie said.

"Come on out, you two. You've got an invite for dinner."

Chapter 18

Conrad and Arturo lifted their hands and shaded their eyes as they hung back in the smokehouse to let themselves get used to the light. Though Conrad couldn't see the big blond man, he was confident Ollie wasn't alone. He figured there were several men with guns pointed at the prisoners.

As his eyes began to adjust and he lowered his hand to squint at their captors, he saw that he was right. Half a dozen men stood outside the smokehouse including Ollie, who held a leveled revolver. Two men had handguns, while the other three weren't taking any chances. They each had 12-gauge Greeners aimed at Conrad and Arturo.

"Come on," Ollie said again, sounding a little impatient. "Dan and Selena are expectin' you. You don't want them to get tired of waitin'."

As they started out of the smokehouse Arturo stumbled a little. Conrad gripped his arm to steady him. "Looks like we're going to dinner," he murmured.

"The condemned men ate a hearty last meal," Arturo muttered back at him.

"What are you two sayin'?" Ollie demanded.

Conrad shook his head. "Nothing important, Ollie. What's your last name, anyway?"

"Barnstabble," the big man answered. "Sort of like barn and stable. I reckon one of my ancestors in England or some such place used to keep livestock."

Arturo nodded. "That sounds like a plausible theory."

"We're going to Kingman's house for dinner?" Conrad asked. He glanced at the sky and saw that the sun was low in the west. Another hour of daylight was left, no more.

"That's right," Ollie said as he gestured with the barrel of the gun he held. "Let's go."

As the group started toward Kingman's cabin, Ollie went on in a confidential tone, "I think it was Selena's idea. She doesn't think Dan's treated you all that good since you joined up with us."

One of the other guards spoke up. "Ollie, if Dan was here I reckon he'd tell you to quit runnin' your mouth so much. And these two fellas haven't joined up with us. They're Gentiles, and they're our prisoners!"

"Yeah, but only until Dan comes to an understandin' with 'em."

"For God's sake." The man pointed at Conrad. "This one busted you in the snoot a few hours ago!"

Conrad could see the bruises his punch had left on Ollie's face. He smiled. "For what it's worth, Ollie, I'm sorry I hit you." Ollie was either slow-witted or just incredibly good-natured, but it didn't hurt to have someone on the other side who was slightly friendly.

"See?" Ollie said. "Mr. Browning just didn't really understand what was goin' on."

The other men exchanged glances. Conrad knew what they were thinking. *Somebody* didn't understand what was going on, but it wasn't Conrad.

They marched toward Kingman's cabin. Conrad saw quite a few people standing around the other cabins watching them with great curiosity. He figured not many outsiders came here, and certainly not many Gentiles.

Kingman was waiting for them and stepped onto the cabin's porch as the group came up. He had a smile on his face, but it didn't reach all the way to his eyes. They were cold and calculating.

"Come in, come in," he said. "I hope the past few hours haven't been too unpleasant. Selena has convinced me I'm being too cautious where you gentlemen are concerned. I thought that to make amends, we'd invite you to break bread with us, then you can leave if you want to. Or you're welcome to stay a few days if you'd prefer."

Conrad nodded. "We appreciate that." He and Arturo would play along, but he didn't trust the man at all.

Kingman said, "Ollie, you and these other fellas can put your guns up and go on about your business. Mr. Browning and Mr. Vincenzo aren't going to cause any more trouble, are you?"

"That's right," Conrad said.

He and Arturo went up the steps to the porch. Kingman stepped aside to hold out a hand and usher them in.

Selena was waiting for them inside. She had changed from the men's clothing she had worn when she fled Juniper Canyon into a nice-looking gingham dress with a square-cut neckline. Conrad figured she had stuffed the dress and a few supplies into the saddlebags along with the money she had stolen from Elder Hissop.

"Hello," she said to Conrad and Arturo with a more genuine smile than the one Kingman had mustered up. "We're so sorry about all the mis-understandings, aren't we, Dan?"

"Sure," Kingman said. "I'd offer you a drink, but we don't indulge in spirits here. We have some nice cool buttermilk, though."

"That would be fine," Conrad said.

"Dinner's almost ready. Why don't we sit down?"

Kingman made it sound like he was enter-taining them in a luxurious parlor in a mansion on Beacon Hill, instead of a log cabin in an isolated valley in the rugged Utah-Nevada border country. To be fair, the cabin appeared to be well built and comfortably furnished with a nice table and several sturdy chairs. A rug lay on the puncheon floor. A couple oil lamps lit the room. Conrad wondered how all those things had gotten there.

Selena poured glasses of buttermilk for them. Conrad, Arturo, and Kingman sat at the table while Selena went back to the stove, where a pot of something that smelled good was simmering.

Conrad took a sip of the buttermilk. "It looks like you've got a nice little community here. Do you plan to stay in this valley permanently?"

"Why would we leave?" Kingman asked. "There's fertile ground for farming, and plenty of graze for cattle. We can live comfortably here."

"I didn't see any livestock when we were riding in."

Kingman shrugged. "We'll put together a herd later on. The first thing we had to do was get the cabins built and establish ourselves here."

That made sense, Conrad supposed, although wondered where Kingman intended to get those cattle. He suspected rustling might be involved. Stealing Father Agony's stock would be one more way of getting back at the elder who had banished the young men.

"There's one other thing most of the men are lacking," Conrad said. "Wives."

Selena turned at the stove. "There are several other women here."

"You can't count on enough of them getting

away from Juniper Canyon like you did, though."

With his mouth set in a tight line, Kingman said, "I'm not sure this is any of your business, Browning. We're trying to be hospitable here."

"Sorry," Conrad said. "Didn't mean any offense."

He didn't care whether he offended Kingman, but he didn't want to upset Selena. She would be upset soon enough when she realized the man she thought of as her husband was a rustler and an outlaw.

Selena dished up bowls of stew with chunks of venison, potatoes, carrots, and wild onions swimming in it and set a plate full of thick slices of bread on the table. Kingman explained they sent out hunting parties for fresh meat. He said grace before they ate, and then everyone dug in. As they were eating, Kingman asked, "Where were the two of you headed when you stopped to help Selena?"

"They were on their way to California," Selena answered. "Isn't that what you said, Conrad?"

He nodded. "That's right. We're bound for San Francisco, but there's no real hurry."

"You have business there?" Kingman asked. He was angling to find out if anyone would miss them if they disappeared, Conrad thought.

"That's right."

"Well, we don't want to keep you. You're free to go whenever you like. The only thing I ask is that you don't say anything to anybody about what you've seen here."

Conrad nodded. "Fair enough."

"You'll be leaving first thing in the morning, then?"

"We'll see."

Selena said, "Dan, it sounds like you're trying to get rid of them. That's not very hospitable."

"I'm just trying not to inconvenience our guests," he said easily, spreading his hands as if his intentions were perfectly honorable and innocent.

Conrad didn't believe that for a second.

The rest of the evening was somewhat awkward. Conrad and Kingman continued being polite to each other, but the tension between them was still there. When the meal was finally over, Kingman said, "I've set aside one of the cabins for you tonight. We can't expect you to sleep in that smokehouse."

Conrad nodded. "We appreciate that, don't we, Arturo?"

"Most definitely," Arturo said. "You rugged frontiersmen may have mastered the art of sleeping on hard ground, but I never have."

"Well, you don't have to worry about that," Kingman said. He pushed back his chair and stood up. "I'll have some of the men show you where the cabin is."

Obviously, dinner was over.

Conrad and Arturo got to their feet. Conrad smiled and nodded to Selena. "Thank you for the meal. It was very good."

"Quite appetizing," Arturo added.

"It's the least we could do, considering how the two of you saved me from being taken back to Juniper Canyon."

Kingman ushered them out. Conrad wasn't surprised to find the same bunch that had escorted him and Arturo earlier, minus Ollie Barnstabble, waiting outside the cabin. He had a pretty good idea what was about to happen.

"Take our guests to where they'll be spending the night," Kingman said as he closed the door behind him so Selena wouldn't see or hear what was happening.

"Sure, Dan," one of the men replied. He had a Greener tucked under his arm.

Conrad and Arturo exchanged a glance. Kingman wasn't going to wait any longer to dispose of them. His henchmen would take the prisoners away from the little settlement, kill them, and dump the bodies in a ravine where they would never be found, or something along those lines. Then they would hide the buggy and Conrad's horse, and in the morning Kingman would tell Selena they had left early, before daybreak, to resume their trip to San Francisco. There might be a part of her that would doubt the story, but she wouldn't be able to do anything about it.

The men carrying the shotguns shifted the weapons and looped thumbs over hammers. "Come on, you two," the spokesman said.

Conrad looked at Kingman and spoke bluntly. "You don't have to do this. We're no threat to you. Whatever you're doing here, it's none of our business."

"I can't take that chance," Kingman said. "Not after we've worked so hard to make a place for ourselves. Not while we're surrounded by enemies on all sides. I'm sorry, but this is the way it has to be." He looked at his men and added in a voice as hard as flint, "See to it."

Chapter 19

Conrad gave a little shake of his head to Arturo. They could raise a ruckus, but all Kingman had to do was yell and dozens of reinforcements would come running. As bad as five-to-two odds were, it could be even worse.

They went down the steps, and the men closed in around them. With shotguns prodding them in the back, Conrad and Arturo marched along the road until one of their captors said, "All right, head up over that hill."

Night had fallen, but there was enough star-light for Conrad to see the tree-covered hill to the left of the road. He angled toward it and trudged up the slope with Arturo at his side.

On the other side of the hill was a little canyon that cut toward the mountains to the south. Once the group entered the canyon, it was hard to see, so one of the men scraped a lucifer to life and lit a torch he had brought with him. With the hill between them and the settlement, they didn't have to worry about the flickering light being seen.

The canyon twisted and turned for about half a mile. Finally, the leader said, "All right, that's far enough."

"When you men followed Kingman over here from Elder Hissop's community, I'll bet you didn't realize you'd wind up being murderers, did you?" Conrad asked.

"Forget it," the leader snapped. "That might work on an idiot like Ollie, but you're not gonna talk us out of doing what has to be done. The valley has to be protected at all costs." The man paused. "Anyway, you're just a couple of Gentiles. After the things your kind has done to us over the years, we won't lose any sleep over killing the two of you."

Conrad heard the men backing off behind them, getting some room so they could use those scatterguns. The man holding the torch raised it higher. The harsh glare from the flames washed over Conrad and Arturo and cast long shadows on the ground in front of them. Conrad tensed, readying himself to whirl around and make a desperate leap for the closest man. One thing about shotguns, they were very indiscriminate weapons. If he could get close enough to one of the men before the others pulled their triggers, they would have to hold their fire for fear of hitting their companions.

Before Conrad could make his move, a voice called, "Hey, what's goin' on here?"

In the split second that followed, Conrad recognized Ollie's voice. The five men jerked their heads around toward him.

Conrad launched himself at the nearest man in a diving tackle and crashed into him. Wrapping his arms around the man's waist he drove him off his feet. The man let out a startled yell as he went down, and the torch flew out of his hand.

Arturo leaped forward and snatched the torch out of the air, then slung it in the faces of the other men. They flinched away from the burning brand, giving Conrad time to yank the pistol of the man he had tackled from its holster. He tipped up the barrel and triggered three fast shots. Two of the men went down.

Arturo charged after throwing the torch. He was no brawler, but he was fighting for his life. He grabbed the twin barrels of a shotgun and wrenched the weapon upward. He and the man who held the Greener staggered back and forth as they wrestled over the shotgun.

Conrad swung the gun in his hand and squeezed off another round. A man howled in pain and dropped his shotgun as he clutched at a bullet-shattered shoulder. That left Arturo's opponent and the man Conrad had tackled, who suddenly grabbed him. Conrad brought the gun barrel down against the man's forehead with a crashing thud, and he went limp again.

Leaping to his feet Conrad rushed toward Arturo and the last man. They were turning around and around as they struggled. Waiting for a second until he had the right opening, Conrad slammed the revolver against the man's skull with stunning force. Instantly, the man let go of the shotgun and his knees folded up. He dropped senseless to the ground.

"Mr. Browning!"

Conrad spun around, hoping the gun in his hand had at least one round left in it. He leveled the gun at Ollie, who came forward into the light cast by the torch still flickering on the ground.

Ollie had his revolver pointed shakily at Conrad. "Mr. Browning, what are you doing? Those are my friends you shot!"

"They may be your friends, Ollie, but they were going to murder Arturo and me."

"Why would they do that?"

"Because Kingman ordered them to."

Ollie shook his head. "Dan wouldn't do that. He's a good man. He wouldn't have anybody killed."

"I think you know better," Conrad said. "I sure wish you'd put up your gun. I don't want to hurt you."

"But . . . but Dan and Selena had you to dinner!"

Arturo said, "That was a façade for Miss Webster's benefit. Knowing that she's fond of us, he wanted to make her believe everything was all right, then he could dispose of us without her ever knowing anything about it."

"Arturo's right, Ollie," Conrad said. "He would have told Selena in the morning that we left early and headed on to California, when actually these men were going to kill us and hide our bodies."

Stubbornly, Ollie shook his head. "This is all crazy."

"You saw for yourself what was going on. They were about to cut us to ribbons with those shotguns. Why else would they bring us all the way out here like this?"

Conrad could see the struggle on Ollie's face. He had cast his lot with Kingman and the others, but being a cold-blooded killer wasn't in his nature. Finally, after a long, tense moment, Ollie lowered his revolver.

"I knew it wasn't right," he muttered. "When Dan had us start holdin' up those trains, I knew it wasn't gonna be the way he said it'd be. He said we'd live here in peace and ever'body would leave us alone, but I didn't know we'd have to steal to do it. Or kill innocent folks."

That was the final piece in the puzzle, Conrad thought. The Outcast Saints really were outlaws, just as he had suspected. The Southern Pacific line wasn't that far. They could hold up a train, then retreat to the valley. Some of the furnishings in the cabins had probably come from those robberies.

"Dan plans on rustling Elder Hissop's cattle, too, doesn't he?" Conrad asked.

Ollie sighed. "I think so. It won't work, though. The elder won't let him get away with it. He'll send out Leatherwood and the rest of the avengin' angels to track us down." He holstered his gun. "I'm startin' to wish I'd never left Juniper Canyon."

"I thought Elder Hissop forced you out. Banished you."

"He banished *Dan*, because Dan and Selena wanted to get married. Dan got some other fellas to go with him. There were plenty who liked certain girls but had to watch while they were married off to the elder's friends. And there were some of us, like me, who came along because our friends were leavin'. Dan and I been pards ever since we were kids."

Conrad heard the pain in Ollie's voice. It wasn't easy, discovering that a longtime friend wasn't really the person he had seemed to be. Whether Dan Kingman had changed, or whether he had always been a ruthless outlaw at his core, didn't really matter. Ollie was seeing him for what he was.

Ollie took a deep breath and blew it out. "You fellas get on out of here. I'll take care of the boys you shot, and I won't raise the alarm until you've had a chance to put some distance behind you."

"You're sending us out on foot?" Conrad asked. "That's a death sentence. As soon as Kingman finds out what happened, he'll come after us, and he won't have any trouble hunting us down."

"I'm givin' you a chance," Ollie said. "That's all I can do. I ain't gonna betray my friends any more than that."

Conrad was considering the odds of agreeing to Ollie's proposal, then circling around and stealing some horses from the settlement, when gunshots suddenly roared in the distance.

Ollie swung around and stared off toward the settlement. "What in the world?"

Shots continued to blast. Conrad's conclusion was inescapable.

War had come to the Valley of the Outcast Saints.

Chapter 20

Arturo held the Greener. Conrad bent swiftly and pulled two more revolvers from the holsters of the men he'd shot. He tucked the guns behind his belt and picked up a shotgun. "Let's go.

Leatherwood and the avenging angels must have found the valley."

It was the first thought that had occurred to him, and as guns continued to go off in the distance, he was convinced it was the only explanation for so much shooting.

"No!" Ollie said. "Leatherwood will kill anybody who gets in his way while he's tryin' to carry out Elder Hissop's orders."

"We know that as well as you do," Conrad told him. "We've swapped lead with him a couple times ourselves."

The three of them ran back down the canyon and up the hill. When they reached the top, they paused to look toward the settlement. Conrad had already noticed an orange glow in the sky, so he wasn't surprised to see flames leaping up. At least one of the cabins was on fire.

He reached out to grasp Ollie's arm as the young man started to rush down the hill. "Wait a minute."

"But those are my friends! I've got to help them!"

"If we go charging in there, Leatherwood and his men will just gun us down, too. Let's figure out what we're going to do before we get there. You know this valley a lot better than we do. Is there a way we can circle around and get back to the settlement without using the road?"

"Well, yeah, there are some other trails . . ."

"Lead the way," Conrad said.

They left the road and trotted through groves of trees and along ridges. Ollie seemed to know where he was going, even though it was too dark to see very well. The shooting began to taper off, and Conrad thought that was a bad sign. When it stopped completely a few minutes later, he *knew* it wasn't good.

They came up behind Kingman's cabin. It was on fire, and even in the trees thirty yards away, Conrad felt the heat of the blaze against his face. The flames cast a large circle of hellish light, and he saw a number of men on horseback. They wore the dusters and broad-brimmed hats of the avenging angels, proof that Jackson Leatherwood had tracked his quarry to the valley.

A second later, Conrad saw Leatherwood himself. It was impossible to mistake that scarred, ugly face. He rode back and forth holding a Winchester pointed upward, the butt propped against his thigh. He wore an arrogant sneer as he surveyed the destruction his men had carried out. A number of bodies lay sprawled in the firelight, and several more Outcast Saints had been taken prisoner and herded together. Heavily armed men on horseback surrounded them.

Ollie drew his gun and started to lift it. Conrad caught his wrist and forced it down.

"Let me go," Ollie said. "I think I can hit Leatherwood from here."

135

"That's doubtful, and even if you did, it wouldn't change anything. The rest of them would just charge over here and kill us."

"I can't let them get away with this!"

"I didn't say anything about letting them get away with it. But we'll have to be smart about it."

Ollie shook his head miserably. "I've never been smart, Mr. Browning. Fact is, I'm kind of dumb."

"Then let me do the thinking for us," Conrad urged. "As it happens, I'm pretty smart most of the time."

It hadn't saved him from the tragedies that had befallen him, he thought . . . but Ollie didn't need to know that.

"Conrad, look," Arturo said. "It's Miss Webster."

A couple dismounted gunmen held Selena, one on each side, and were forcing her toward Leatherwood. As they came to a stop in front of the leader of the avenging angels, Selena screamed hysterical curses at him, words a good Mormon girl shouldn't have known. Leatherwood sat there and took it for a moment, then slid his rifle back in the saddle boot and swung down from his horse. His hand came up and cracked across Selena's face with such force the blow would have knocked her down if the two men hadn't been holding her.

Ollie made a growling sound deep in his throat. Knowing exactly how the big man felt, Conrad wanted to charge out there himself and smash a fist into Leatherwood's face, then plant a bullet in the man.

Conrad reined in his anger and said quietly, "Take it easy. Leatherwood's time is coming."

"Not soon enough for me." Ollie's voice trembled with rage.

Leatherwood said something to his men and made a curt gesture. They dragged Selena away. He mounted up again, and a moment later one of his men rode up with Selena astride his horse, in front of the saddle, his arm tight around her. Leatherwood called out an order, and the avenging angels galloped out of the settlement, taking Selena with them but leaving the stunned survivors of the attack behind. Conrad was a little surprised Leatherwood hadn't ordered them executed. Maybe he figured he had wiped out enough of the Outcast Saints that they weren't a threat anymore.

"Now what do we do?" Ollie asked.

"Come on," Conrad told him. "Some of those men may be wounded and need help."

As they came out the trees, the roof of Kingman's cabin collapsed, sending a huge shower of sparks high, lighting up the sky. One of the men spotted Conrad, Arturo, and Ollie approaching.

"It's them!" the man yelled. "The outsiders! They led Leatherwood here!"

The men surged toward Conrad and his companions. Angry muttering came from them, and Conrad knew it wouldn't take much for them to turn into a vengeance-crazed mob.

Ollie stepped in front of Conrad and Arturo and held up his hands. "Hold it! You can't blame this on these men. *We* brought them here. Leatherwood followed *our* trail from that camp down by the railroad."

"Why are you defending them, Ollie?" one of the survivors demanded. "They're Gentiles!"

"Yeah, but they haven't done anything wrong. All they ever did was help Selena, and for that . . . for that—" Ollie's voice choked off. He still didn't want to admit Kingman had tried to have Conrad and Arturo murdered.

Conrad stepped forward. "Listen to me. I'm going after Leatherwood. He has to pay for what he's done here tonight. If anybody wants to come with me, you'll be more than welcome. But I'm settling the score with Leatherwood, one way or another."

More muttering came from the men, but it wasn't as angry. Finally one of them stepped forward. "They didn't just take Selena. They took my Rachel, too, and the other women we had here. Took them back to Father Agony and his cronies. I don't like you, mister, but if you think you can help us get them back . . . I'm willing to go along with you."

A couple other men nodded.

But another man spoke up, saying, "Not me. I'm done with this. Dan Kingman said we'd start our own community here where everyone would be treated fairly, but all he did was turn us into a bunch of outlaws! I don't want any part of any of it anymore."

Conrad nodded. "Anybody who feels like that is free to go." He sensed that by the sheer force of his personality, he had taken control of the situation, as he had so often in the business world, back in that other life of his. He had been able to walk into a room filled with men hostile to what he wanted, and before he was finished, he was giving them orders.

Four men were willing to go after Leatherwood, while five refused. Ollie told them, "There are some of our boys up in that little canyon on the other side of Cedar Hill. Some of them are wounded and need help."

"What happened up there, Ollie?" one man asked.

Ollie hesitated. "Dan sent them on an errand, and it didn't work out. You don't have to come with Mr. Browning and me, but the least you can do is give those boys a hand before you leave the valley."

The men agreed to do that.

Conrad said, "We'd better see about getting some horses ready to ride—"

"Leatherwood's men busted down the corral fence and scattered the horses. They're all over the valley by now."

Conrad was disappointed to hear that, but he said, "Then we'd better start looking for them. We can't afford to waste any time if we're going to catch up to Leatherwood before he and his bunch get back to Juniper Canyon."

He was about to turn away when one of the men exclaimed, "Oh, my Lord! Look at that!"

Conrad saw where the man was staring and swung around to look in the same direction. He was shocked to see a figure stumbling toward them. The man's clothes were charred tatters, and his skin was blistered in some places and covered with soot in others. Conrad had no trouble recognizing him, though.

Dan Kingman was still alive.

Chapter 21

Conrad's hands tightened on the shotgun he held. He didn't believe in taking chances.

Kingman appeared to be unarmed, and judging by his shambling gait, he was somewhat disoriented. He came to a stop in front of the men and stared at them, not seeming to comprehend what he was looking at.

Ollie took a step toward him and held out a hand. "Dan? Are you all right?"

Kingman flinched away for a second, then shook his head. He didn't seem to be saying "no" to Ollie's question. It was more of a clearing-the-cobwebs gesture.

"Ollie?" he muttered. Then he looked past the big blond man and focused on Conrad. "Browning!"

"Take it easy, Kingman," Conrad said.

Kingman's blistered face twisted in a scowl. He lurched forward a step and raised his hands. "You did this! You brought Leatherwood here!"

Ollie got between Conrad and Kingman, just as he had with the other men earlier. "Hold on, Dan," he said in an urgent voice. "That's not the way it is. We're the ones who left the trail up here to the valley. We made Mr. Browning and Mr. Vincenzo come with us, remember?"

"The avenging angels never found this valley before!"

Conrad said, "Maybe they never looked all that hard until Selena ran off with Father Agony's money. Maybe they didn't really care where the rest of you went."

"Selena!" Kingman croaked, as if he had just thought of her. He swung around to stare in wide-eyed horror at the burned-out cabin. "Selena!"

Ollie hurried to grab him as Kingman started toward the cabin. "She ain't in there, Dan! Do you hear me? Selena's not in there. But she's all right. We saw her just a little while ago."

Kingman sagged in Ollie's grip in obvious relief at that news. He looked around. "Then where is she? Is she here?"

"I'm sorry, Dan . . . Leatherwood took her."

Kingman turned his head to stare up at Ollie. "Took her? You mean—"

"By now the avenging angels are on their way back to Juniper Canyon with Selena and the other women who were here. But we're going after them," Conrad said.

"Going after them? You mean to get her back?"

Conrad nodded. "Her and the other women."

"And to see that Leatherwood has his just desserts meted out to him," Arturo added.

Kingman took a couple deep breaths, then looked up at Ollie and nodded. "You can let go of me now. I'm not out of my head anymore. I'll be all right." As Ollie released him, Kingman turned his attention to Conrad. "I'm coming with you."

"First tell me how you managed to survive that fire."

Kingman's chin jutted out defiantly. "I don't have to explain anything to you."

"Well, I'd sure like to know, too," Ollie said. "When I saw your cabin burnin' up like that, and you weren't out here with the other fellas, I figured for sure you were in there and were a goner."

Kingman continued to glare at Conrad for a second before he shrugged and said to Ollie, "I almost was. I think we're wasting time talking about this, but . . . When the shooting started I ran outside to see what was going on, but there were so many bullets flying around I had to retreat into the cabin. Anyway, I wanted to protect Selena. A couple of Leatherwood's men managed to bust through the door before I could stop them, and one of them slugged me with a rifle butt." He touched his head. "He was going to shoot me, but the other one stopped him. Said they ought to burn the cabin down around me, that Elder Hissop would like that. He said . . . he said I was going to wind up burning in the pits of Hell anyway, so I might as well start by burning here."

Visibly overwhelmed by the horrible memory, Kingman dragged in a shaky breath before he could go on.

"That's the last I heard before I passed out. When I came to, I thought I was already in Hell, all right. There was fire all around me. My clothes were on fire. I realized I was still in the cabin and made it to my feet. Part of the back wall was already burned through. I had to jump through the flames, but managed to get out that way. Then I fell down and rolled around to put out my clothes, and I started to crawl away from the fire. I guess I passed out again. I woke up . . . a few minutes ago . . . behind what's left of the cabin. We've wasted enough time. We need to get started after Leatherwood."

"What you need is some doctorin'," Ollie said. "You got burns all over you, Dan."

Kingman shook his head stubbornly. "I don't care about that. What happens to me doesn't matter. It's Selena—"

"The avenging angels scattered the horses. It's going to take some time to round them up. While we're doing that, you can get those burns tended to. I'm sure somebody here knows how to take care of injuries like that. Find some clothes that aren't half burned off you, too." Conrad looked around at the men who were going after Leatherwood. "We'll all need guns. Where's my buggy?"

"We parked it in the barn. It should be all right."

Conrad nodded. "I've got a couple extra pistols in my gear, if we need them. Ollie, you make sure Kingman gets some medical attention."

Ollie nodded. "Sure thing. I can take care of that myself."

While Conrad was speaking, Kingman stared at him. As shaken up as he'd been by his narrow escape from the fire, Kingman hadn't realized Conrad and Arturo shouldn't be there. He wondered why they were still alive . . . and how things had worked out that Conrad was giving orders.

Men scattered to look for the horses, and Ollie said, "Come on back to my cabin with me, Dan. I got some salve we used to use on Elder Hissop's cattle when we'd brand 'em. I reckon it might work for burns like this, too."

"Wait a minute." Kingman stepped away from him and confronted Conrad. "Listen, Browning—"

"Whatever you're going to say, I don't want to hear it," Conrad said. "And I'm sure as hell not interested in offering explanations for anything that might be puzzling you. Let's just say your plans didn't work out the way you expected, and from here on out, all I'm interested in is getting Selena away from those lunatics who have her now. Are we clear on that?"

Kingman stared at him for a moment, the anger in his eyes fading until he finally nodded. "Yeah. We're clear. And whatever you can do to help her . . . I appreciate it, Browning."

"No thanks necessary," Conrad snapped. "Go with Ollie. I want to see if I can find my horse."

Gingerly, Ollie took hold of one of Kingman's burned arms and led him away toward the cluster of cabins. As they watched the two of them go, Arturo said to Conrad, "Do you believe that young Mr. Kingman's change of heart is genuine?"

"I'm not going to count on it," Conrad said. "I still don't trust him."

"Nor do I." Arturo slid his fingertips along the smooth stock of the shotgun he held. "I believe I'm going to appoint myself the task of keeping a close eye on the gentleman."

Conrad gave him a weary smile. "Sounds good to me. Let's go find those horses."

Chapter 22

Conrad knew they couldn't go after Selena without horses, but the delay while they searched for the stampeded animals caused worry to gnaw at his thoughts. He hoped he'd be able to locate the black gelding because he knew how strong and dependable it was—but would take any mount he could find.

As it worked out, the first horse he and Arturo found was a roan that shied away until Conrad spoke to it in a calm, soothing voice as he approached. He had learned the trick from his father, and it nearly always worked. They had brought a couple bridles with them, and as soon as he was within reach, Conrad slipped the leather harness over the roan's head. The horse fought halfheartedly, and Conrad figured it was probably glad to have a human calling the shots again.

He handed the reins to Arturo, who led the roan while they continued looking for another horse.

A few minutes later, Conrad heard some racket in a thicket of brush. He took a chance and let out a low whistle. The noise stopped. He whistled again, and a large, dark shape pushed itself out of the thicket with a crackle of branches. The horse gave a familiar toss of its head. Conrad grinned as he recognized it. "It's good to see you, too," he told the black as he came up to it and slipped the bridle on.

"Since we have our full allotment of horses, I suppose we should head back to the cabins now?" Arturo asked.

"Yeah, but we'll keep our eyes open along the way. If we find any more, we'll try to drive them that direction." Conrad paused. "How are you at riding bareback?"

"Bareback?" Arturo repeated, sounding as if he could hardly believe Conrad had asked the question. "Completely inexperienced and vaguely horrified at the mere concept. Riding with a good saddle is perilous enough to the male anatomy. But I suppose if you insist . . ."

"No, no, we'll lead them. Come on."

They didn't see any more horses on their way back to the settlement, but by the time they got there, three of the men who had agreed to come with them had arrived not only with mounts for themselves but several extras. The fourth man showed up a short time later with two horses. Taking saddles and tack from the barn they got the animals ready to ride.

Kingman and Ollie came back from Ollie's cabin. Kingman wore jeans, a flannel shirt, and a pair of high-topped boots. They weren't Ollie's, that much was certain. Ollie's clothes would have swallowed Kingman whole.

Along with the fresh clothes, Kingman had a gunbelt strapped around his hips with a black-butted Colt in its holster. He carried an old Henry rifle. Conrad smelled a pungent odor coming from him and figured it was that cow-doping salve Ollie had mentioned.

"All right, I'm here," Kingman said. "I just need a horse."

Conrad had already put a saddle on the roan for Arturo, and was tightening his own saddle on the black. He leaned his head toward the spare mounts. "Take your pick, but you'll have to be fast about it. The rest of us are ready to ride."

"Listen here, Browning, I don't know what makes you think you can give orders—"

Kingman's angry response stopped short as he made a visible effort to control himself. Clearly, he didn't like the fact that Conrad seemed to have taken charge of the rescue effort, but they had called an implied truce earlier.

Conrad hoped that was what caused Kingman to rein in his temper. It might be the man was just biding his time, taking advantage of Conrad's offer to help rescue Selena, all the while plotting how he could double-cross Conrad and Arturo later, once Selena was safe.

That was assuming they were able to rescue her, Conrad thought . . . and the odds against that were pretty long.

"How many of us are going?" Kingman asked while Ollie saddled a couple of the remaining horses.

"Eight."

Kingman frowned. "Is that all? What happened to the rest of the men who survived the raid? There were more than six of us, weren't there?"

Ollie looked uncomfortable. "They've, uh, decided they don't want to stay here anymore, Dan. They're gonna move on."

"And let Leatherwood get away with what he's done?" Kingman asked in a mixture of outrage and disbelief.

"That's their decision to make," Conrad said. "Are we ready to go?"

He looked around at the members of the group. All of them nodded except Kingman, who put his foot in the stirrup and swung up into the saddle. He kicked his horse into a run.

Conrad and the others mounted and followed at a slower pace.

Ollie said worriedly, "Dan doesn't need to be runnin' that horse so hard. It'll play out, and then he'll be stuck."

"That's his problem," Conrad said. "He's smart enough to realize what he's doing is stupid. If he keeps it up, he'll have no one to blame but himself."

And Kingman having to give up the chase would be a mixed blessing, Conrad mused. On the one hand, not having Kingman with them meant they'd have one less gun.

On the other hand, it also meant Conrad wouldn't have to worry about Kingman shooting him in the back during a battle with the avenging angels.

By the time they reached the pass, Kingman had stopped to wait for them. "I guess I lost my head a little back there. We've got to push ourselves pretty hard, or else we won't catch up to Leatherwood before he gets back to Juniper Canyon."

"I think the odds of that are already pretty slim," Conrad said. "Having to take the time to catch the horses gave them a good lead on us. Unless Leatherwood stops and makes camp for the night, I don't think we'll catch him."

"He won't do that," Kingman said. "He'll be too anxious to get back to Father Agony and deliver the prize to him. He knows where he's going, so he'll ride on through the night."

Conrad nodded. "I agree. And *we* know where he's going, so we don't have to worry about following any trail they leave behind. We can head straight for Juniper Canyon."

"Then let's do it." Kingman heeled his horse into motion, holding it down to a lope.

The eight riders moved through the pass and started down the twisting trail on the other side. It took them back into the dry, inhospitable country that most of the region was like. A three-quarter moon had risen, and its silvery glow reflected off the impassible salt flats to the east, creating a white gleam that lit up the night almost like day.

Kingman gradually pulled ahead again. Ollie brought his mount alongside Conrad's and said quietly, "I'm worried about something, Mr. Browning."

"What's that?"

"Even if we catch up to Leatherwood before he gets back to Juniper Canyon—and I know, that ain't likely to happen—we'll still be out-numbered. If we don't catch up, that means we'll have to rescue Selena and the other women from Elder Hissop's fort, and he'll have a lot more men to fight us than just Leatherwood and some avenging angels, so it'll be even worse."

Conrad looked over at Ollie. "Fort? Nobody said anything about a fort."

"Well, it's not like a cavalry fort or anything like that. It's more like a big house, I guess you'd say, where Elder Hissop and all his family live. He's got seven wives already, you know, and there ain't no tellin' how many kids. I can't keep up with that, but Father Agony's old enough that some of his sons are grown men and more of 'em almost are, and they'll fight for him. They'll do anything he tells them to, you can count on that, because he sees to it they get first call on all the women he don't want for himself. Then you've got some brothers and cousins and nephews thrown in, and some fellas who ain't related by blood but might as well be, they've been followin' the elder for so long. You might almost say he's got himself an army. Since they can hole up in that big house with its thick adobe walls and a parapet on top where he puts riflemen, it just seems natural that you could call it—"

"A fort," Conrad said. "I see your point, Ollie."

"I'm as anxious to get those gals back as anybody, but there's just eight of us. Eight. I'm startin' to wonder just what it is we can do."

"Well, that's the thing about a fort. It can be strong enough to keep out an army, but rats can still get in there. That's what we may have to be."

"Rats?"

"That's right." Conrad nodded. "Well-armed rats."

Chapter 23

By the middle of the next day, Conrad and his companions had seen no sign of the men they were after. It had become obvious they weren't going to catch Jackson Leatherwood. He had to be pushing his avenging angels as hard as the pursuers were pushing themselves.

Realizing that, Conrad called a halt to rest their horses.

Kingman reined in, but he hipped around in the saddle to complain. "We're wasting time by stopping now. These horses can go a little farther." He had voiced the same complaint each time they had stopped to rest the horses.

Conrad was getting tired of it. "What's the earliest we could make it to Juniper Canyon even if we didn't stop again? Sometime tonight?"

Ollie and a couple men nodded and muttered agreement. "It'd be midnight or later even if we were able to ride straight through," Ollie said.

"In that case, I don't see any point in wearing out our horses—or killing them—in an attempt to get there sooner," Conrad went on. "That would just leave us a lot worse off."

Kingman sighed and dismounted. "You're right, I know. I just can't stop thinking about Selena being their prisoner."

"Leatherwood's not going to let anything happen to Selena before he gets her back to Hissop. He'll want to deliver her safe and sound. I think you can be pretty sure of that."

Ollie spoke up again. "Those avengin' angels are killers, Dan, but they wouldn't mistreat a woman."

One of the men said, "And Selena's not the only prisoner. My Rachel is with them."

"And my Dora," another man said.

"And my Caroline," a third put in.

"I know. I'm sorry," Kingman said. "I don't

mean to slight anybody. We'll rescue all the women, of course."

At least Kingman genuinely seemed to care about Selena, Conrad thought, and wasn't just upset because of the two thousand dollars he had lost at the same time. He had become an outlaw after he was banished from Juniper Canyon, but still had *some* human feelings.

Of course, Conrad had a hunch Kingman would try to recover that loot, along with rescuing the women. If it came down to deciding between Selena and the money, Conrad had little confidence in which one Kingman would choose.

As they continued along the railroad Conrad spotted the water tank at Navajo Wash. Each man had a canteen slung on his saddle, but in the hot, dry country a single canteen didn't last all that long. Between the men and the horses the water supply was already running low. It was a good chance to top off their canteens.

He remembered water spraying out through the bullet holes in the tank where Leatherwood's men had shot it. If a train had come along since then and stopped to take on water for its boiler, the train crew likely had noted the problem and patched the holes. Even if that wasn't the case, the tank would still have water in it below the level of the bullet holes.

"Kingman, we're going to stop up ahead at Navajo Wash," Conrad called.

Riding in front as usual, Kingman glanced around as if he were going to argue, but then he nodded. No matter how upset he was, in country like this a man never lost track of how much water he had left and where he could get more. If he let himself get too distracted and forgot about those things, nine times out of ten the buzzards wound up picking his bones.

The riders moved on toward the water tank. Conrad found himself staring at it, thinking about the furious gun battle he and Arturo had fought there a couple days earlier against the avenging angels. It seemed more like ages had passed since then.

It was hard to keep track of things when people were trying to kill you all the time, he told himself with an inward chuckle. After a while, all the deadly days started to run together.

Sunlight suddenly winked off something on the tank. A nail head, maybe, or some sort of metal strap?

But the reflection moved, bouncing against Conrad's eyes again from a slightly different position, and he knew it wasn't any nail head.

"Spread out!" he shouted as he kicked the black into a run. "Everybody spread out!"

Arturo reacted instantly. He had done a good job learning the lessons that traveling with Conrad Browning taught a man. He veered his horse in the opposite direction from Conrad's and urged it into a hard gallop.

The Outcast Saints were a little slower to move. The whipcrack of a rifle shot sounded from the water tank, and one of the men grunted, jerking back in his saddle. He managed to stay mounted, but sagged forward over his horse's neck and dropped the reins. The horse spooked and bolted ahead in a run.

Seeing their companion shot prodded the other men into frantic action. They followed the example set by Conrad and Arturo and raced off in all different directions, no longer easy to cut down.

Conrad leaned forward in the saddle as he rode. Drawing his Winchester from its sheath he watched the water tank. He could see one man up on the platform. No, more than that, he corrected himself as more shots rang out. Two or three at least, and men were firing from behind the shed.

Leatherwood had split his force. Though the avenging angels had left their surviving enemies defeated and demoralized, he knew there was a chance they would mount a pursuit. He had left men at Navajo Wash to ambush anyone who came after them, to make sure he reached Juniper Canyon with the prizes he had claimed for Father Agony. It was good strategy.

The rescuers would have to fight, and they had already suffered an injury. Maybe a fatality. Conrad had lost sight of the wounded man.

He crossed the tracks and circled to the left of

the water tank. Guiding the black with his knees, he levered a round into the Winchester's chamber and fired at the tank. The back of a galloping horse was no place for accuracy, so he didn't try to be too fine about his shots. He cranked off half a dozen rounds as fast as he could, spraying the platform.

The tank would have more holes in it before the day was over.

It wasn't the only thing with holes. One of the ambushers flew backward off the platform with his arms flailing. From that distance, his scream was a tiny little thing, cut short in a hurry as he crashed to the ground on his back.

Conrad flashed past the tank. He felt the hot breath of a slug as it passed close to his cheek, but that was the closest any of the bushwhacker lead came to him. He could see the men behind the shed, so he circled back toward the tracks to get a better shot at them.

With a flash of pride he noted Arturo coming in from the other side. He had the heart of a warrior, although he would have denied that. He was willing to fight and pitched in without hesitation. Conrad saw smoke spurting from the muzzle of Arturo's rifle.

Kingman had chosen a different tactic, plunging straight ahead along the tracks. He had almost reached the tank without being shot, when he hauled back on his horse's reins so violently the animal skidded to a halt and reared up on its hind legs, pawing at the air.

His revolver barked twice, and another man clutched at his belly and spun off the platform. Diving out of the saddle as the last man on the platform fired down at him at almost point-blank range, he rolled into the shadows under the tank, and that was the last Conrad saw of him for the moment.

One of Leatherwood's men behind the shed was down, but two others were still on their feet, firing. Conrad's heart leaped into his throat as he saw Arturo's horse stumble and fall, but Arturo was thrown clear. He crashed to the ground, rolled over a couple times, then lay still. He was an easy target.

Before anyone could draw a bead on the fallen man, Ollie Barnstabble came charging around the shed on his horse. He left the saddle in a dive and threw his arms out like the wings of a giant bird, embracing both gunmen and driving them off their feet. One man rammed head-first into the shed wall and collapsed. The other one tried to put up a fight but was no match for Ollie's size and strength. Ollie dragged him to his feet and shook the fight—and possibly the life—out of him.

Arturo pushed himself to his hands and knees but was slow getting up. Since the three men who'd been behind the shed were taken care of,

Conrad sent his horse galloping toward Arturo, as he heard a swift flurry of gunshots. Glancing back he saw the third and final gunman topple from the platform. Kingman had finished him off.

Conrad was out of the saddle and off the black before the horse completely stopped moving. Taking hold of Arturo's arm he helped him to his feet. "Are you all right? Were you hit by any of those bullets?"

Arturo was wheezing and gasping. "Just . . . just got the breath . . . knocked out of me, sir. I'll be . . . fine . . . in a moment."

Conrad looked him over and didn't see any bloodstains on his clothes. "You were splendid just now, you know," he told Arturo with a smile.

"Thank you, sir. What about the others?"

"Let's go see." Conrad took the reins of both horses and led them toward the shed and the water tank.

Ollie stood over the sprawled bodies of the three men by the shed. "They're all dead," he reported without Conrad having to ask him. "One shot and a couple with busted necks."

"The three who were up on the platform are done for, too," Kingman put in as he thumbed fresh rounds into the cylinder of his Colt. "All of them drilled."

"What about our man who was wounded?"

Ollie grimaced. "If we get Dora back, she's gonna be a widow. Come to think of it, I guess she's a widow anyway, whether we get her back or not, because Todd's dead. Looked like that shot got him through the heart, the poor fella."

"So now there's seven of us," Kingman said as he snapped his gun closed. "The odds just got worse. Although they were so bad to start with I don't reckon it really matters."

"It matters," Conrad said. "It'll matter to Dora." He looked at the bodies sprawled on the ground. "I don't suppose anybody thought to bring a shovel?"

Chapter 24

No one had a shovel, but they were able to use a broken board from the shed to gouge out a grave for Todd. Ollie, with his massive muscles, did most of the work.

The bodies of the avenging angels were left where they had fallen. Conrad was tired of wasting time and effort on fanatical, cold-blooded killers.

Once Todd was laid to rest, the group moved on quickly. They found the horses ridden by Leatherwood's men hidden in Navajo Wash and took the six animals with them. Extra mounts always came in handy, and they would need horses for Selena and the other women when they made their escape from Juniper Canyon.

Conrad didn't think Leatherwood would divide his forces any more than he already had, so another ambush was unlikely. Conrad warned his companions to remain alert anyway. Anything was possible.

He recognized the spot where he and Arturo had first encountered Selena when she was being chased by Leatherwood and his men. But he didn't know how to get to Juniper Canyon from there, so he would have to rely on the others to lead the way.

Kingman, Ollie, and the other three Outcast Saints had been born and raised there. It must have been hard to leave the only home they had ever known, Conrad thought.

He had spent most of his childhood in Boston, although there had been trips to Europe. When he was older his mother had taken him with her when she traveled across the country to check on her business interests. It had been during one such trip that Vivian Browning had been reunited with Frank Morgan, and Conrad had learned who his father really was.

Heading north, away from the railroad, Conrad's group rode the third leg of the giant U-shape enclosing the terrible salt flats with Juniper Canyon on one side and the pass leading to the Valley of the Outcast Saints on the other. By nightfall they hadn't reached the mountains where Agonistes Hissop's stronghold was located, but they pushed on anyway, sipping from their canteens, gnawing on strips of jerky they had brought with them, stopping to rest the horses occasionally. The long, hard, dangerous day had left them gaunt, grim, and for the most part silent. Conrad's companions reminded him a little of wolves, even Arturo and big, friendly Ollie. He was sure he probably looked the same to them. Weariness sat heavily across his shoulders.

The dark, looming bulk of the mountains drew steadily closer as the stars wheeled across the sky. The moon rose, arced across the heavens, and started its descent. The mountains appeared as far away as ever, then suddenly, they were looming over the seven riders like sleeping giants.

Kingman reined in and pointed. "There. That's the mouth of Juniper Canyon."

They stopped, and Conrad said, "Tell me about the place."

"What do you want to know?" Some of his natural surliness crept back into Kingman's voice.

"The terrain, how the canyon is shaped, how the community is laid out, that sort of thing. The things I'll need to know if we're going in there, rescue the women, and make it back out alive."

"I'd still like to know—" Kingman stopped with an abrupt shake of his head. "Never mind. The canyon. Let's see. The mouth of it is fairly narrow, maybe a quarter mile wide, and it stays like that for a couple miles as it runs up the mountains. It's the only real gap for miles in the long ridge that forms the edge of the mountains."

"Does it run straight?"

Kingman nodded. "For the most part. There are a couple little bends but no real turns. Then it opens out into a big basin at least a mile across. There's a spring right in the middle of the basin that forms a pool in the rocks, and that's where Elder Hissop settled some forty years ago." Kingman gave a bitter laugh. "He always says he'd been wandering in the desert and an angel led him there, delivering him from certain death. I used to believe that story, but now I know that no self-respecting angel would have anything to do with Father Agony."

"There are juniper trees growing around the pool," Ollie put in. "That's how the place got its name. And junipers on the slopes all around the canyon, too."

"How steep are those slopes?" Conrad asked.

"Pretty steep on the way in. A horse would have a hard time gettin' up and down 'em. At the end of the canyon, where the settlement is, they're not so bad. There's decent graze in the hills all around . . . well, decent for this part of the country, I guess you'd say . . . but not as good as we've got in our valley. The elder keeps his cattle up in those high pastures and grazes his sheep down in the basin, where the grass isn't as good."

"What about the settlement itself?"

Kingman said, "Hissop's house is the closest to the pool, since it was the first one built there. And it's a monstrosity. He built it for him and his original wife and kept adding on as he added wives and children. It's adobe, two stories in some parts and three stories in others. The tallest part is a blasted watchtower he built on top of it. The roofs are flat, so he can put riflemen up there, and there are walls to give them cover. I remember when I was a kid and the Paiutes would go on a rampage, everybody in the community would go to the elder's house for safety while the men fought off the Indians. The savages never got in. Never came close. Eventually they gave up and quit trying."

"I told you it was a fort," Ollie added.

"What about the rest of the houses?"

"Scattered all over the place," Kingman said. "Along with barns, corrals, a blacksmith shop, a saddlery, a mill, a couple grain warehouses, and things like that. Most of them are built of adobe, but there are some log cabins, too. The men who are Hissop's long-time followers, the ones who are members of his inner circle, I guess you'd say, have the best houses and the houses that are closest to Father Agony's."

"Sounds like everything in the place revolves around him," Conrad commented.

Kingman nodded. "That's exactly the way it is. He was supposed to be our leader in living according to God's teachings, but somehow it got to be about worshipping *him,* although he'd call you a blasphemer and set Leatherwood and the avenging angels on you if you ever dared to say such a thing."

"You sound like you're speaking from experience," Conrad said.

Kingman shrugged. "I had my share of run-ins with Father Agony even before I knew he had his lecherous sights set on Selena. I guess it was inevitable there'd be a showdown." He grunted. "And inevitable who would win, too. If I had stayed, Leatherwood or one of Hissop's other triggerites would have gunned me down."

Arturo said, "I've heard this word *triggerite* used several times, but I don't think I've ever encountered the term before now. I assume it means the same thing as a gunman?"

"Yeah," one of the Outcast Saints said. "It comes from that song about Porter Rockwell."

"Who?"

"His name is Porter Rockwell, heeee's the Mormon triggerite," Ollie sang softly in a deep, surprisingly rich voice.

"Don't start on that," Kingman said. "Rockwell wasn't just an avenging angel. People called him the Destroying Angel. He was the personal bodyguard to Joseph Smith and to Brigham Young. If they wanted somebody dead . . . well, that fella usually wound up dead, and everybody knew Old Port was responsible. If you ask me, Leatherwood's always wanted to be as famous as Porter Rockwell, and it gnaws at his gut that he's not."

Conrad had vague memories of hearing about Porter Rockwell in the past. He wondered if Frank Morgan had ever crossed trails with the man. Conrad wouldn't doubt it for a second. The Drifter's decades of wandering across the frontier had brought him in contact with just about everybody who was famous or notorious.

Hearing about Porter Rockwell was interesting but not relevant to why they were there. To steer the conversation back along more useful lines, Conrad said, "If the terrain around Hissop's stronghold isn't that rough, we ought to be able to get in that way instead of going straight up the canyon."

"Nope." Kingman shook his head. "Not from this direction. The country on the other side of the ridge isn't that bad, but the ridge itself is too steep and rough. You couldn't get horses over it. To get in from the other side you'd have to circle so far around it would take you days, maybe even a week." Kingman's voice took on a bleak edge. "We can't leave Selena in Hissop's hands for a week. If we do, she'll be his wife by then, if she's not already."

"Then we'll have to go straight up the canyon after all. I assume Hissop keeps it guarded?"

"Some of Leatherwood's men are always on watch."

"Then we'll need to take care of them somehow. You said men could climb the ridge and make their way along it?"

Kingman nodded. "That's right." A note of eagerness came into his voice. "We could get behind them that way. I know where they camp to watch the entrance. Leatherwood sends men in groups of three out there for several days at a time. Two of them are always on guard while the other one sleeps."

"How do they signal the stronghold if there's trouble?"

"They fire off some shots."

"Then we'll have to be fast and quiet and make sure they don't get a chance to do that."

"We?" Kingman repeated.

"I think it's a job for two men," Conrad said, "and whether we like it or not, you and I are the ones best suited to the job."

Chapter 25

In only a few hours it would be dawn, so there was no time to waste once Conrad had figured out what to do. Kingman insisted he knew every foot of the ridge, even in the dark, having explored it hundreds of times when he was a boy.

"There'll be three guards," Ollie said as Conrad and Kingman got ready to go. "I ought to come with you so the odds'll be even."

Conrad shook his head. "One of the men will be asleep when we get to their camp. We'll have to handle the other two quickly enough that we can be ready for him when he wakes up."

Conrad didn't add that Ollie was too big and clumsy to move with the stealth that would be necessary. There was no need to hurt the young man's feelings.

"Once we've taken care of the guards, I'll come to the mouth of the canyon and signal the rest of you," Conrad went on. "It'll be fast, so watch close for it. I'll strike a match and hold it in front of my body where it can't be seen from inside the canyon. I'll pass my other hand back and forth in front of it three times. When you see that blinking light, bring the horses to the canyon. Don't waste any time, but try to be as quiet as you can. It's likely sound travels well up the canyon at night."

"We understand," Arturo said. "What then?"

"Somebody will wait with the horses where the canyon opens into the basin while the rest of us head for Hissop's house to look for the women. If we can sneak in and get them out of there without anybody knowing, that's fine, but there's a better chance we'll have to fight our way back to the horses. When we get there we'll mount up and try to make it back to the valley on the other side of the salt flats before Leatherwood can catch up to us."

Kingman said, "If we can get there, we can hold the pass, even if we just have a small force. We might even be able to close it, if we have time to prepare some charges." He looked at Conrad. "You know about things like that. What do you think?"

"A well-placed blast or two would probably drop enough rock in the pass to close it," Conrad agreed. "But you'd never be able to use it again. Is there another way out of that valley? I didn't see one, but I never really got a good look at it."

"I don't know if there is or not," Kingman admitted. "I haven't explored the whole place. But even if we can't leave . . . why would we want to? You saw it. It's paradise on earth! At least as close to it as you're going to find in this part of the country. Maybe we ought to call it Paradise Valley. We could live out our lives there and be happy."

Conrad had serious doubts about that. He figured the contentment Kingman expected to find would last for a while, but it wouldn't be permanent. Nothing was, and every bit of paradise he had ever seen had turned, sooner or later, into hell.

He shook off the thought. "That might be all right for you, but Arturo and I can't stay there. We have business elsewhere. We'd have to get out before you blow the charges."

"That could put you at Leatherwood's mercy."

Conrad shrugged. "We'll have to run the risk." He glanced at Arturo. "But maybe I should speak for myself. Arturo, you might want to stay in Paradise Valley."

"Good heavens, no," Arturo replied without hesitation. "No offense to you gentlemen, I'm certain you'll have wonderful lives there, but my place is elsewhere. Also, we're putting the proverbial cart before the hypothetical horse here, are we not? We have yet to penetrate Juniper Canyon, let alone rescue Miss Webster and the other ladies and make our escape with them."

Conrad laughed. "Good point. Everybody clear about what we're doing?"

The rest of the men nodded.

"All right." To Kingman he said, "Let's go."

As they moved off on foot, Arturo called softly behind them, "Good luck, sir."

Conrad figured they would need it.

He let Kingman take the lead. The base of the ridge was almost sheer, but after looking around a bit Kingman found a narrow trail they were able to use. It was little more than a series of footholds and handholds, and Conrad saw that Kingman had been right: a horse would never be able to maneuver up and down the trail.

The slope eased, so they were able to walk

rather than climb, but it was still rugged. A giant rock slab barred their path at one point, forcing Conrad to boost Kingman to the top, where Kingman stretched out and extended a hand down to Conrad to help him up. Looking at the ridge, it didn't seem to be that tall and intimidating, but getting to the top seemed to take forever. Conrad worried too much time was passing. They needed darkness if they were going to have any chance of getting in and out of Elder Hissop's house without getting caught.

Eventually they came out on top of the ridge, which was a couple miles wide, composed of jagged clefts and pinnacles. In the moonlight, it looked like alien landscape, like several other places he had been recently, Conrad thought. He was sure he had never come across country as downright inhospitable as that corner of Utah. The vast, barren ugliness made the occasional oasis seem idyllic.

As the two men paused to rest for a moment, Conrad said, "Are you sure you know your way through this maze? It looks like a man could wander around in it forever."

"I can get through it," Kingman said confidently.

"All right. I don't have any choice but to trust you."

"That's right. You don't." Kingman jerked his head toward the north. "You ready?"

"Yeah."

"Then let's go."

They set off again. Kingman led the way around spires of rock and across chasms spanned by narrow, natural stone bridges. It was a harrowing path, especially in the dark, but the moon and stars provided enough light for Conrad to see where his companion was going, and he was careful to step in the same places Kingman stepped.

After less than an hour, Kingman held up a hand in a signal to halt. He leaned close to Conrad and whispered, "We're almost there. We'll have to climb down, but it's not too bad. When we get to the floor of the canyon, there'll be some trees to our left, about two hundred yards away. That's where the guards' camp is. We'll work our way along the wall toward them. We'll be behind them, so they shouldn't see us coming, but be careful anyway."

"I intend to," Conrad whispered back.

Kingman nodded. He moved ahead, and a few minutes later, they reached the rim of the canyon.

The ground dropped away. Stunted junipers grew out of the steep slope, demonstrating how stubborn and hardy they were. The sharp tang of their scent filled the air. Conrad watched as Kingman turned around and backed over the edge, then began climbing down between the trees, catching hold of a protruding root here and there to steady himself.

Conrad followed in the same way, moving slowly and deliberately. The canyon wall wasn't sheer. He would probably survive a tumble, but it would cause a racket, alerting the guards, and *that* could certainly prove fatal.

When his boots touched the canyon floor Kingman was waiting and pointed at the dark cluster of trees that was their objective. Conrad nodded. They set off toward the trees, using every bit of stealth at their command.

As they soundlessly approached the camp, Conrad heard two men talking together in quiet voices. Kingman stopped and pressed himself against the trunk of a juniper, and Conrad followed suit, figuring Kingman wanted to eavesdrop on the conversation for a moment before they struck. They might find out something important.

The two guards were having a mild argument about the proper way to shear a sheep. Conrad didn't think he and Kingman were going to learn anything useful, but the sheep-shearing discussion led to the subject of mutton, and he heard "Do you think there'll be any at the wedding feast?"

"Of course. There'll be a little of everything at the feast, I expect. Elder Hissop's so excited to be marrying the Webster girl, he wants a big celebration."

"I'm glad our turn on guard will be over this morning. I'd hate to miss it."

So Hissop hadn't forced Selena to marry him as soon as Leatherwood brought her back to Juniper Canyon. Good to know, Conrad thought. But the wedding would be soon, no doubt about that.

"You don't think that Kingman boy will show up, do you?" the second guard asked.

"He'd be a fool if he did. Brother Jackson will kill him on sight. Of course, in the long run it won't matter. Kingman and all the rest of those Outcast Saints are doomed. Elder Hissop wants the avenging angels to go back over there and clean out that nest of sinners."

"About time," the other man agreed.

Given what they had just heard, Kingman's idea of blowing up the pass and sealing off the valley wasn't so far-fetched. It might take that to prevent his community from being wiped out. Conrad had his doubts about how well it would work out, but that might be the only alternative.

First, though, they had to survive the rest of the night and the day to come, by taking care of the guards. Conrad's eyes had adjusted well enough to the shadows under the trees that he could see the two men sitting on a log next to a cold fire pit. To one side was a tent where the third guard was sleeping. Conrad heard faint snores coming from inside the tent.

To Conrad's left, behind one of the trees, Kingman drew his gun and nodded. Conrad's

Colt was already in his hand. He returned the nod. The plan was to knock out the guards, tie them up, and gag them. They would do the same to the third guard.

Just as Conrad and Kingman moved into the open, one of the guards suddenly stood up and turned around, saying, "I need to—"

Whatever need he was about to express went unspoken as he spotted the shadowy forms sneaking up on them. He opened his mouth to yell, and jerked up the rifle he held.

Chapter 26

In the dead of night, the sound of a shot would carry easily to the settlement at the other end of the canyon, two miles away. That knowledge gave Conrad speed as he flung himself forward, his left hand closing around the rifle barrel. Instead of wrenching the weapon out of the guard's hand, which would have caused it to go off, he shoved as hard as he could, driving the stock into the guard's belly. The man grunted in pain, doubled over, and let go of the rifle.

Conrad swung the revolver in his hand and smashed its barrel against the man's head. The guard dropped instantly and didn't move when he hit the ground.

Kingman had leaped forward with matching

swiftness. The second guard barely had time to react when Kingman's gun crashed against his head and knocked his hat flying. The man crumpled.

The commotion roused the third guard. He burst out of the tent with his suspenders flapping around his hips and ran right into Conrad's hard fist, which caught him solidly on the nose. Cartilage crunched and blood spurted as the man's nose flattened, and he went over backward. As soon as he hit the ground, Kingman finished the job with a sharp rap from his gun butt. The man sighed and stretched out in a limp sprawl.

Conrad and Kingman holstered their Colts. A second later, Conrad saw a reflection of moonlight on steel and realized Kingman had drawn a knife. As he bent toward the unconscious men, Conrad said quietly but sharply, "What are you doing? We were just going to fix it where they couldn't raise the alarm."

"I guarantee they won't make any racket if their throats are cut," Kingman said.

"Hold it. You're too quick to resort to murder to make sure people don't cause problems for you, Kingman."

"Blast it, this is none of your business!"

"As long as I'm risking my life and the life of my friend to help you, it is. Kill those men in cold blood and you and Ollie and the others are on your own. Arturo and I are riding away."

"You're awful high and mighty." Anger seethed in Kingman's voice. "You never did anything that was over the line, Browning?"

Conrad remembered several times he had pulled a trigger in cold blood and ended the life of an evil man. The thing of it was, he had *known* the evil those men had done. Maybe these guards were guilty of things just as bad. Whether that was the case or not, he didn't have any knowledge of it himself, and he wouldn't stand by and watch them slaughtered like sheep while they were uncon-scious and helpless.

"We said we'd tie them up and gag them, and that's what we're going to do."

"Fine!" Kingman jammed his knife back in its sheath. "We're wasting time."

Conrad couldn't argue with that. He and Kingman worked quickly, using the mens' belts to tie their hands behind them, ripping strips from their shirts to lash their ankles and knees together, and stuffing bandannas in their mouths as gags. They dragged the unconscious men deeper into the trees and left them there.

While Kingman looked up the canyon to make sure no one else was around, Conrad hurried to its mouth, about fifty yards away from the guards' camp, and dug a lucifer out of his pocket. He snapped it to life with his thumbnail, and moved his other hand back and forth in front of it in the signal he had told the others. He blew out the match and ground it under his boot heel.

A couple minutes later he heard the steady *thud-thud-thud* of approaching hoofbeats. Shadowy shapes came into sight. "Conrad?" Arturo called quietly.

"Here."

Arturo, Ollie, and the other three men led the horses up to the mouth of the canyon. "Kingman's scouting the other way, but it should be all clear," Conrad told them. "Come on."

He led them into the canyon, where they met Kingman trotting back toward them a few minutes later. "Everything's quiet and peaceful, as far as I can tell," he reported.

"All right," Conrad said. "Lead the way."

"You can't get lost," Kingman said. "There aren't any side canyons or anything like that. But I'll go first."

They moved at a deliberate pace so as not to make much noise with the horses they were leading. It took three-quarters of an hour to reach the other end of the canyon. Once again Conrad worried that too much time was passing, that the sun was going to come up soon, but hurrying could be disastrous. He had to be patient, which wasn't always an easy thing for him.

They stopped a couple hundred yards before the canyon widened into the basin where the settlement was located. "Who's staying with the horses?" Kingman asked. "And you'd better not say that I am, Browning, because I'm telling you right now—"

"Take it easy," Conrad said. "Arturo, you're staying."

"I'm perfectly willing to come along and shoulder my share of the risks," Arturo said.

"I know that," Conrad told him. "But we also need somebody dependable to keep up with these horses. We're liable to need mounts in a hurry when we get back here."

Arturo nodded. "Yes, that does seem to be an important job. All right. I agree. It's the logical thing to do. I'm probably not as proficient at violence as these other gentlemen . . . although Lord knows circumstances have forced me to become more so than I ever thought I would be."

"Life has a way of doing that," Conrad agreed. He turned to the others. "Where will Hissop have Selena and the other women? What would he consider proper, since he's going to be marrying her soon?"

"Selena would have been returned to her father," Kingman said. "I can show you the house."

"What about the other women?"

One of the men said, "They'll have gone back to their families, too. They're all promised to some of Father Agony's cronies. That's why they ran away to start with. Their fathers will have the job of keeping them under control until those weddings can be set up."

"Then you know where to look for them," Conrad said. "Can you get into the houses?"

"Just try and stop us," the man said grimly as he rested a hand on the butt of his gun.

"Don't get trigger-happy," Conrad warned. "A bunch of shooting will rouse the whole settlement. Ideally, what you'd like to do is get in and rescue the women without anybody even knowing about it. If that's not possible, don't shoot unless you absolutely have to."

Ollie said, "I've got an idea. Instead of us splittin' up, why don't me and these three fellas all go together to each house where one of the gals is bein' held? That way if there's trouble, we can all handle it. And I'm big enough I can usually stop trouble before it really starts, if I do say so myself."

Conrad grinned. "Ollie, that's an excellent idea. The four of you gather up the other women, Arturo will take care of the horses, and Dan and I will go after Selena."

"What about Leatherwood?" Kingman asked in a tight voice. "You said we were going to get vengeance on him. And on Hissop."

"What's more important? The lives of the women and the lives of your friends, or vengeance?"

"We can't let them get away with the things they've done," Kingman insisted.

"If we get those women away from them, I

think there's a mighty good chance you'll have an opportunity to deal out some revenge to Leatherwood and Hissop," Conrad said. "They're not going to let you ride away with Selena and the other ladies."

"That's true," Kingman admitted with a shrug. "And I know you're right, the most important thing is rescuing the women. I just hate to miss a chance to kill those two like the low-life snakes they are."

"Speaking of Leatherwood," Conrad said, "where do he and the other avenging angels stay while they're here in Juniper Canyon?"

"Their quarters are in a long, low adobe building next to Hissop's house."

"So if there's any trouble at the elder's, they'll be handy."

"That's right."

"Where does Selena's father live?"

"A little farther away, in another adobe house."

"We can't count on a racket going unheard by the avenging angels, then," Conrad mused.

"Not really."

"Then I guess we'd better not make any more racket than we have to." Conrad looked around at the men. "Anybody think of anything else?"

They shook their heads.

"I guess we're ready to go, then." He looked at the sky. "There's maybe an hour and a half until it'll be light enough to see. We need to be out of here before then if we're going to have any chance to get away. Good luck."

Several of the men echoed that sentiment.

They started off at a trot through the darkness. Conrad hesitated just long enough to shake hands with Arturo, then started after Kingman. He never went into something thinking he wasn't going to survive, but he knew that possibility always existed. It was definitely a lion's-den situation. Elder Hissop had a couple hundred devoted followers at his beck and call, ready to help him with whatever trouble he had, and about three dozen of them were avenging angels, fanatical triggerites who would just as soon kill a man as look at him. Conrad had six desperate young men. Those were pretty piss-poor odds, Conrad thought. They went beyond piss-poor. They were downright suicidal.

But he and his companions had come too far to give up. Too much was at stake.

He caught up to Kingman as they reached the end of the canyon. Even in the bad light, Conrad saw the slopes falling away and the land in front of him opening up into that basin. Compared to other basins, like the Humboldt in Nevada, it was tiny, just a speck in a vast, rugged landscape. But it was a whole world to the people who lived there. He was an interloper, Conrad thought, who had no real right to be interfering with their lives . . .

Other than the certain knowledge that Agonistes Hissop and Jackson Leatherwood were evil men who had evil plans, somebody had to put a stop to those plans, and it looked like that was going to be up to Conrad and the men who had come with him.

A number of paths branched out from the trail that ran through the lower part of the canyon. Kingman took one leading toward the center of the basin. As Conrad trotted along beside him, he saw what appeared to be cultivated fields, as well as orchards and pastures where herds of woolly sheep grazed and moved around sleepily.

"Are the fields irrigated from that spring you mentioned?" he asked.

"Yeah," Kingman said. "Hissop put in a series of aqueducts and irrigation ditches all over the basin. He has a steam-powered pump that pumps water to the ditches, as well as some windmills. He's a smart man, I'll give him that. Makes him even more dangerous when you're going up against him."

Conrad understood. An intelligent enemy was always worse.

Kingman stopped short, touched Conrad's arm, and pointed. "There. That's Father Agony's fort."

It was deserving of the name, Conrad saw as he peered through a gap in the trees. The big house stood several hundred yards away on a slight knoll that gave it a view of the large, calm pool formed by the spring and surrounded by rocks. Junipers grew all around the house, which, as Kingman and Ollie had said, had a bizarre look to it because of the way it had been enlarged over the years. Wings ran off at all angles, at different lengths and heights, sprouting from the main, original part of the structure like the legs of a spider from its body. In fact, Conrad thought, if you looked at the house from above, it might even resemble a fat, deformed spider that had stopped scuttling along through the Utah landscape and squatted there motionless, waiting to trap any unwary insects that ventured near it.

Not a very comforting thought, he told himself with a shadow of a smile.

"Does he keep guards in that watchtower all the time?" Conrad asked.

Kingman shook his head. "Not unless things have changed since I was banished. He puts guards up there only when he's expecting trouble."

"Like now, since he stole Selena back from you?"

"Oh. Yeah, there might be guards up there. Stay behind cover as much as you can, especially when we're sneaking up on the Webster house. It's close enough that anybody on the tower could see us without much trouble."

"What about the Webster house?"

"It's just a regular adobe ranch house, about a quarter mile east of Hissop's fort. We can circle around behind it and keep the house between us and Hissop's while we approach."

"Sounds good." Conrad nodded. "Let's go."

No lights appeared to be burning in the house as they moved silently toward it. Suddenly, dogs began to bark somewhere else in the basin, and Conrad wondered if the other men had run into trouble. More dogs started carrying on, as dogs always will, and within a minute or two it sounded like every dog in the basin was barking.

"This is good," Kingman whispered. "If old Soames Webster hears his hounds barking, he'll think they're pitching a fit because every other dog around here is."

It might be a lucky break for the two of them, all right, Conrad thought. He still worried about Ollie and the others, but concentrated on his own mission. "Selena never said anything about having any brothers. Will there be any men in the house besides her father?"

"She doesn't have any brothers. Webster had only the one wife, Selena's mother. Never wanted any others, or so he claimed. And after Selena was born . . . well, I guess her mother couldn't have any more children or something. She was the only one. That made her pretty unusual."

"I imagine." Conrad knew Mormons were noted for their large families.

"Being unusual made Hissop want her even more, I think. He's always regarded her as special, even when she was a child."

They came to a stop behind the house. As Kingman had said, it was a typical, low-ceilinged, flat-roofed adobe ranch house. Thick beams known as vigas protruded along the upper edges of the walls. A shaded, arbor-like portal was set in the center of the building.

"The kitchen is inside that door," Kingman whispered. "Selena's room is to the right. Her father's room is the other way, at the left front of the house."

"Unless Webster's changed things around in case somebody tries to sneak in and get her."

Kingman grunted. "You're giving the man credit for too much intelligence. Webster never had a thought in his head that Father Agony didn't have first." He started forward. "Come on."

Conrad catfooted along behind Kingman. The young man had just reached the door and was about to pull the string that would open the latch when light suddenly blazed up all around them. Men with torches had lit them and stepped around both corners of the house, and the reddish glare washed over Conrad and Kingman, blinding them for a moment.

Conrad could hear just fine, though, so he had no trouble hearing the deadly *clack-clack* of Winchester levers being worked, followed by a honeyed purr of a voice declaring triumphantly, "See, brethren, how the Lord has delivered the evildoers right into our hands?"

Conrad knew without being told that the voice belonged to Elder Agonistes Hissop.

Father Agony.

Chapter 27

Despite the glaring torchlight, from the corner of his eye Conrad saw Kingman reach for a gun. His hand shot out and closed around Kingman's wrist, stopping the draw before it could really begin. Half blind, surrounded by riflemen, slapping leather would only get them shot to pieces. That wouldn't help save Selena or anybody else.

"Easy," Conrad said. "They'll kill you."

"You're blessed right we will," a familiar voice rumbled. It belonged to Jackson Leatherwood, Conrad realized. The leader of the avenging angels was somewhere behind the light. "Sooner or later, we'll kill you no matter what you do, you heathens, so you might as well go ahead and reach for your irons now and get it over with."

"Now, now, Jackson," another voice scolded. "There's no need to gloat, simply because we have emerged triumphant from our travails with these young men. You gentlemen drop your

weapons, please. Carefully. Use your left hands."
It was Hissop.

Kingman glanced at Conrad. A muscle jumped in his tightly clenched jaw.

"Better do what he says," Conrad warned. "This isn't over."

Hissop chuckled. "Listen to your Gentile friend, Daniel, but be advised he's wrong about one thing. This is most definitely over."

Conrad reached with his left hand and slid the Colt out of its holster. He leaned over and placed the revolver on the ground. Beside him, Kingman sighed and followed suit. He dropped his knife on the ground next to the gun.

Once the two of them were disarmed, several men hurried forward. They wore the wide-brimmed hats and long coats of avenging angels, but Conrad didn't recognize any of them. He figured the men would grab them and hustle them off to wherever Hissop intended to lock them up, but without warning, one of the men rammed a rifle barrel in his belly. Conrad doubled over in pain. Another man kicked his feet out from under him. The same thing happened to Kingman. As the avenging angels closed in around them, Conrad thought they intended to stomp the life out of him and Kingman.

Instead, the men stopped, then the circle parted. Conrad lifted his head. Jackson Leatherwood came through the gap first and looked down at the prisoners with a sneer on his ugly face, making it even uglier. Then Leatherwood stepped aside to allow the much smaller man to regard Conrad and Kingman with a solemn expression.

The man was in his late fifties or early sixties, with a slightly round face and wispy white hair. Unlike most of the Mormon elders, he was clean shaven. He wore a sober black suit and a string tie. His mild demeanor and small stature made him seem harmless at first glance, but Conrad saw the madness burning in his pale blue eyes.

"You men have caused me a great deal of trial and tribulation," Hissop said. "I cannot tell you how much it saddens my heart to see that you still oppose the will of the Lord, Daniel."

"It's not the Lord's will I oppose," Kingman said through teeth gritted against the pain of getting hit in the stomach. "It's yours!"

"I am the voice of heaven on earth," Hissop replied calmly. "My will *is* the Lord's will." He looked at Conrad. "As for you, young man, I expect nothing but heresy and blasphemy from an unbeliever, and you have not disappointed me. Unlike some of my faith, I bear no ill will toward Gentiles, but I cannot allow your sins to go unpunished. You made a bad mistake when you cast your lot with this defiant young sinner."

"I was just trying to help a young woman," Conrad said.

"Help her to do what?" Hissop shot back. "To

fly in the face of everything that is divine and holy? The will of the Lord will not be thwarted . . . *and neither will mine.*"

"We'll take them out and kill them, Elder," Leatherwood said.

Hissop shook his head. "No! I will give this boy one more chance to repent of his sins." Hissop hunkered on his heels next to Kingman. He took hold of Kingman's chin and wrenched his head up. "You will attend my wedding to Selena Webster and witness her being joined to me by God. What happens after that will be up to you. You can renounce your sins by joining in the praise of this holy union, in which case you will save not only yourself but also those poor young men you deluded into following you. Or you can remain defiant, and I will have no choice but to order that all of you be put to death."

"You'll . . . save the others?"

"They will escape the fate that would be theirs otherwise, yes. You have my word on it."

"And what about Browning?"

It surprised Conrad that Kingman would give him any thought.

"He is a Gentile," Hissop said. "His sins go far beyond anything in my power to pardon. For the crime of killing our brethren, he must die. But I will see to it his death is quick and pain-less."

Kingman looked over at Conrad and swallowed.

"And all I have to do is . . . give my blessing to your marriage to Selena?"

"That is correct," Hissop said.

"Elder . . ."

"Yes?" Hissop purred as he leaned closer to hear what the young man had to say.

Kingman spat in his face. "Burn in hell, you old toad!"

A split second later, the toe of Leatherwood's boot smashed into Kingman's side, half lifting him off the ground and making him groan in pain. While he lay there whimpering, Hissop straightened. Slowly and with great dignity, he drew a handkerchief from his pocket and wiped the spittle from his face. He nodded to Leatherwood, who kicked Kingman again.

"You have sealed your fate," Hissop intoned as he threw the handkerchief on the ground next to Kingman. "But before you die, you will watch the woman become my bride." He jerked a hand toward Leatherwood. "Take them both and put them with the others."

At least some of the other men had been captured, too, Conrad thought. That came as no surprise. Clearly, Hissop had been expecting them to show up and probably had set up traps at the homes of the other women. Conrad had known from the start that was a possibility, but he had hoped they could rescue the women before Hissop had a chance to put such a plan into action.

The avenging angels reached down, grabbed Conrad and Kingman by the arms, and hauled them to their feet, being none too gentle about it. They were marched toward Hissop's house, then the group turned aside and shoved the prisoners toward a large barn. Torchlight revealed the barn was built of roughly sawn planks. More torches burned inside.

Ollie and two other men were next to a parked buckboard, tied to the thick posts that supported the roof. They were bruised and bloodied and their clothes were torn. Clearly, they had been ambushed and beaten, too. The fourth man wasn't there. Conrad wondered if he had been killed during the struggle.

Ollie let out a groan when he saw Conrad and Kingman. "Aw, Dan, I was hopin' you and Mr. Browning got away with Selena."

Leatherwood smashed a fist across Ollie's face. "Shut your heathen mouth," he growled. "Don't sully the name of Elder Hissop's new bride."

Riflemen surrounded them, so there was no chance to try anything as Conrad and Kingman were thrust up against posts and lashed into place. The men who tied the ropes made sure to jerk the knots cruelly tight. Conrad felt his hands go numb almost instantly.

When the avenging angels were satisfied the prisoners weren't going anywhere, they stepped back. Hissop had followed them into the barn and he stood before the group of captives. "You other men should know you'll be dying because of Daniel Kingman's refusal to repent of his sins. It's too late to save any of you."

"It's always been too late," Kingman said as his head hung forward and he panted for breath. "From the first time any of us . . . dared to stand up to you . . . you made up your mind to kill all of us. It's the only way you can . . . hang on to your power."

"My power has been bestowed upon me by the Lord God Almighty and cannot be taken away by you or anyone else," Hissop declared. "Just as Joseph Smith was visited by the angel Nephi, I, too, was visited by divine messengers who delivered unto me the knowledge and the strength to wrest this piece of heaven from a godforsaken wilderness!" He flung out his arms to indicate their surroundings in the basin. "You cannot oppose the will of God and His prophet without paying the ultimate price!" Hissop turned to Leatherwood and snapped, "Guard them closely. I don't want anything happening before the wedding this afternoon."

"I understand, Elder," Leatherwood replied.

Hissop stalked out of the barn. Leatherwood picked out four of his men and told them to stand guard over the prisoners. Then he and the rest of the avenging angels left. Clearly, there were preparations to be made before

Father Agony could take Selena as his latest bride.

"What happened to Thomas?" Kingman asked quietly when everyone was gone except the guards. "Is he dead?"

"I sorta wish he was, and I hate to say that," Ollie replied. "The rest of us put up a fight when Leatherwood's men jumped us, but Thomas surrendered and talked Elder Hissop into forgivin' him."

"How did he do that?" Kingman asked in obvious amazement.

"He promised to go with Leatherwood back to our valley, on the other side of the salt flats. Leatherwood's gonna go over there and burn down all our cabins and kill anybody he finds still there."

"Betrayed . . ." Kingman muttered. "It's all gone now. Nothing left."

But there was still one sliver of hope remaining, Conrad thought as he stood against the post where he was tied.

That hope's name was Arturo Vincenzo.

Chapter 28

Conrad knew it was a crazy thought, but Arturo wasn't with the prisoners, and no one had said anything about him, so it was possible he was still somewhere in the vicinity of Juniper Canyon, still free. If everything had gone as planned, Arturo would have waited where he was with the horses until Conrad and the others came back.

But things hadn't gone as planned, and Arturo might have realized that. In which case, if he saw some of the avenging angels coming to look for the prisoners' horses, he might have abandoned the animals and fled up the side of the canyon to go into hiding. That notion wasn't so far-fetched.

The far-fetched part was hoping Arturo could do something on his own to save them.

Despite the times when he had risen to the occasion, Arturo wasn't a fighting man. He never would be. It simply wasn't his nature. Against a couple hundred enemies, he would stand no chance at all. He would be doing good merely to survive for a little while.

But where he couldn't outfight the avenging angels, maybe he could outthink them. If Arturo could figure out where Conrad and the others were being held, and somehow free them, they might still be able to fight their way out of Juniper Canyon and make a run for the Valley of the Outcast Saints, where they would make their final stand against Father Agony and his followers.

If wishes were horses, Conrad thought bitterly. The odds against Arturo being able to pull off something like that were so small as to be practically nonexistent.

A dawn wind sprang up outside, gusting through the open doors of the barn and whipping up a swirl of dust that stung Conrad's eyes and nose. It bothered the other prisoners as well, but tied up as they were, there was nothing they could do about it.

The guards pulled their bandannas up over their mouths and noses, protecting them from the dust then moved farther into the shelter of the barn, but remaining close and alert.

Conrad watched the yellow light grow outside and knew the sun was coming up, shining through the pall of dust hanging in the air. He looked over at Kingman and asked quietly, "Do you get storms like this very often?"

"Windstorms, you mean?"

Conrad nodded.

"This isn't a storm," Kingman said. "This is just a little blow. Sometimes the wind howls for days on end, and the dust is so thick in the air you can barely see your hand in front of your face. This is nothing."

Maybe so, Conrad thought, but it might be enough to come in handy by serving as a distraction for the avenging angels, just in case Arturo was skulking around somewhere. It was a faint hope, but Conrad was going to cling to whatever he could.

"Ollie," he said, keeping his voice low enough the guards wouldn't hear it over the wind. "Ollie, have you seen any sign of Arturo?"

"You mean the Italian fella?" Ollie shook his head. "Not since we left him earlier. You reckon they caught him?"

"If they had, chances are they would have put him with us. I think he might still be loose out there somewhere."

Kingman looked and sounded skeptical. "Even if he is, what good can he do for us? He's just one man, and not much of one, at that."

"That's what you think," Conrad said.

"Don't try to give these men hope when there isn't any," Kingman snapped. "It's bad enough I've gotten you all killed. Don't make it worse."

"We're not dead yet," Conrad pointed out.

Time dragged. The heat in the barn rose as the day went on. Beads of sweat popped out on Conrad's forehead and trickled into his eyes and over his cheeks. He blinked them away and forced himself to look around the barn, trying to figure out if there was anything that could be useful in case of a fight. He saw a couple pitchforks and knew their sharp tines made wicked weapons. Through an open door he spotted a pair of shovels and a hoe, along with some other tools like hammers and a keg of nails. A number of boards leaning against the wall in the storeroom were probably used to patch the barn where horses kicked holes in the walls.

Saddles and tack were stored behind another open door, and several ropes hung on nails near the door of the tack room. The barn had more than a dozen stalls, but only four of them held big, stolid-looking horses that probably formed the team for the buckboard.

A bit of a puzzlement was a large, folded piece of canvas that had been painted in bright blue and white stripes. "What's that?" Conrad asked Ollie. "Looks like a piece of a circus tent."

"That's part of the old canopy that used to hang over the brush arbor for shade," Ollie explained. "Elder Hissop replaced it a while back. He had it stored in here, and folks cut pieces off it now and then when they need some canvas. It's a sin to be wasteful, the elder says."

Kingman grunted. "Like that's the only sin Father Agony has to worry about."

He spoke too loudly. One of the guards heard him and came over wearing a scowl. "Don't you disrespect the elder that way," he ordered. "The things you young heathens have done already are bad enough."

Kingman sneered at the man. "What are you going to do? Hissop wants me alive until after that fake wedding of his."

"There's nothing fake about the elder taking a new bride according to the teachings of the Lord. And as for what I can do—" The man slammed the butt of his rifle against Kingman's ribs. "How's that?"

Kingman jerked under the blow and turned pale. Conrad thought he heard a bone crack. The way Leatherwood had kicked Kingman earlier, it wouldn't surprise him if Kingman already had some cracked ribs. Kingman sagged against the ropes holding him to the post and groaned.

The avenging angel grinned arrogantly and strode back to his companions.

The wind had died down and the dust began to settle. Bright afternoon sunshine spilled through the open doors. Conrad was intensely thirsty, and his empty belly told him it had been a long time since he'd eaten. The day was slipping away. How much time did they have left? When was the wedding going to take place?

Jackson Leatherwood stalked into the barn. He nodded to his men. "Have they given any trouble?"

"How can they?" one of the guards replied. "They can't go anywhere or do anything."

"Just the way I like them," Leatherwood responded with a twisted smile.

He sauntered over to the prisoners. "Your time

is just about up. The wedding procession will begin soon, and when it's over, so will your sinful lives be."

"What's Hissop going to do?" Kingman demanded. "Have us killed right in front of Selena? I'm sure that'll make her come to love him."

"You let the elder worry about what his plans are. I'm sure whatever he does, it's because God tells him to. And whatever I do, it's because the elder tells me to. You see how it all works, Kingman? Nice and simple, just the way it's supposed to be."

"That would be fine if Hissop really talked to God. But he's insane. He's not interested in doing what's right, he is only interested in his own power."

"And just how do you know that, eh?" Leatherwood asked. "Maybe you think *you're* a prophet. Maybe you think the angels come and speak to you."

Kingman shook his head. "No. The angels don't talk to me. I'm just a man, a man who's made some terrible mistakes in his life." He glanced at Conrad. "A man who wishes he could get a second chance, so maybe he could undo some things." He sighed. "But there aren't many second chances in life, are there?"

A harsh laugh came from Leatherwood. "A disbeliever like you doesn't even deserve a first chance." He turned and added over his shoulder, "Enjoy the time you've got left, Kingman. There won't be much more of it."

The wind had begun to blow again. Conrad noticed it whipping around the long tails of Leatherwood's duster as the avenging angel left the barn. The light wasn't as strong outside as it had been earlier and the air began to taste of grit.

"Where will they have that wedding?" he asked.

"In the arbor," Ollie replied. "Or in Elder Hissop's house."

The arbor would be better, Conrad mused. Easier to get to. He hadn't given up all hope of getting free somehow, although the chances were getting slimmer and slimmer. If the weather didn't cooperate, the wedding would be moved indoors, which would make things a lot more difficult.

He was thinking about that when instinct made him glance up. He couldn't see into the loft from where he was, but he could hear, and suddenly he heard a faint noise from up there. The scrape of a foot, maybe. It wouldn't be unusual for someone to be up in the hayloft, but the ladder leading to it was only a few feet away from Conrad and he knew no one had gone up there all day.

Then what was it he'd heard? A rat? Sounded mighty heavy to be a rat, he thought.

Conrad tipped his head back and looked up again.

He saw an eye peering back at him through a knothole in one of the loft's floorboards.

Chapter 29

Conrad's heart slugged hard in his chest as he recognized that eye. It belonged to Arturo. He had no idea how Arturo had gotten up there in the loft, but the hope he'd clung to all day finally had a chance to pay off. A chance was all he asked for.

Arturo looked through the knothole for a few seconds, then Conrad heard something move again over his head, something heavy. If he hadn't been listening for it, he wouldn't have heard it over the sound of the rising wind. He looked at the guards. They seemed oblivious to the fact that someone was in the loft.

Arturo looked through the knothole again. He seemed to be trying to tell Conrad something. He wished there was some way they could talk, but that was out of the question. He thought furiously. He had heard Arturo moving something heavy around up there. Well, he asked himself, what would you find in a hayloft that was heavy?

Bales of hay, of course.

Conrad could see it in his mind's eye. Arturo had shoved several bales of hay over to the edge of the loft. They would make effective weapons if he could drop them on the heads of the guards.

The problem was getting the guards to stand where the hay would hit them when it fell.

"I can't take this anymore," Conrad said abruptly. "Hey! Hey, you avenging angels!"

"Browning, what are you doing?" Kingman asked.

"I'm not going to die because of you," Conrad snapped. "This whole mess is none of my business. I never should've gotten mixed up in it in the first place. Hey, guards!"

One of the men strolled over to grin at him. "Quit raising such a ruckus. There's going to be a wedding taking place soon. You don't want to disrupt it."

"The hell I don't," Conrad said. "Tell Elder Hissop I'm sorry, that I'll do whatever he wants me to do. I'll even become a Mormon if that's what it takes. But I don't want to die!"

"You should've thought of that before you killed some of our brethren," the guard said as his face hardened angrily. "It's too late for you to ask for forgiveness, mister. Blood calls out for blood."

"But it was all a mistake!" Only one of the men had come in range. That wasn't enough. Conrad began writhing against his bonds. "You've got to let me go! Please!"

The spectacle of him humiliating himself drew two more guards over to stand in front of him and grin at him. That left just one of them standing near the door. Better odds, maybe the best they could get. But Conrad figured he could try a little harder.

He began to sob.

Tears ran down his face as if his nerve had broken completely. Kingman stared at him in disgust. Ollie looked surprised and disappointed. "Mr. Browning, you really oughtn't to carry on so. . . ."

"I can't help it. I don't want to die! Somebody help me, please!"

The fourth man came over to join the others in gloating.

"Someone," Conrad cried. "Someone from above—"

A large, heavy bale of hay fell from the loft, plummeting down to smash solidly onto the head of one guard and strike a glancing blow to another. The second pair of guards didn't have time to do anything except glance up in surprise before another bale came crashing down on their heads, knocking them off their feet. The bales broke on impact and scattered hay all around the sprawled bodies of the guards.

Arturo jumped down from the loft, holding a pitchfork. He landed on top of one man and plunged the tines into his chest. The hay bales had stunned two guards, but the last man was struggling up and clawing at the gun on his hip. He had dropped his rifle when the hay knocked him down.

Conrad kicked out as far as he could reach. The toe of his boot hit the man's wrist and sent the gun in his hand flying. Arturo pulled the pitchfork free from the chest of the man he had just stabbed and whirled toward the fourth man. He drove the razor-sharp tool into the guard's belly. Tearing it loose as the man collapsed, and before the two men who had been stunned could regain their wits, he dispatched them with the pitchfork, too.

When Arturo turned to face Conrad, his eyes were wide and staring hysterically. For a second he thought Arturo was going to stab him with the pitchfork, too, but then he dropped it, stepped back, and passed a hand over his eyes.

"My God," he said in an awed tone. "My God, what have I done?"

"You've saved our lives, that's what you've done," Conrad said. "Now cut us loose, quick."

Kingman and the other men looked amazed. "Did you know he was up there?" Kingman asked.

"Don't worry about that," Conrad snapped. "Come on, Arturo. That guard's got a knife on his belt. Get it and cut us loose."

"Of course. Of course." With a visible effort, Arturo shook off the horror he felt and stooped to pluck the knife from its sheath. He cut Conrad's bonds first, then tried to press the knife into his hands.

Conrad shook his head as he flexed his fingers.

"My hands are still too numb to handle the knife. You just keep doing what you're doing."

"Very well. I hope I don't cut anyone."

"Don't worry too much about that," Kingman told him. "Just get these ropes off us."

Conrad kept working his hands, getting the feeling back into his fingers as fast as he could. He watched the barn door. No one came near it. Outside, the wind still blew. An idea began to form in his head. As soon as his hands worked again, he stripped the gunbelt off one of the guards and buckled it on, then hurried over to that big folded piece of canvas.

"Give me a hand with this," he told Ollie, who was loose. "Let's put it in the back of the buckboard."

"What for?"

"No time to explain. Just do it. We'll need that keg of nails, a hammer, a couple boards, and some rope, too."

He could tell Ollie was baffled, but the big man did as Conrad asked.

Meanwhile Conrad picked up a fallen rifle and went over to the door, where he looked out carefully. Kingman joined him.

"See anybody moving around?" Kingman asked.

Conrad shook his head. "Not yet. Everybody must be going to that wedding. Where's the arbor from here?"

"About half a mile in that direction." Kingman pointed. "Behind Hissop's house."

"Will all the men be armed, even though it's a wedding?"

"Leatherwood and the avenging angels will be. They always are. The rest of the men probably won't be."

"That's good. We won't have to fight our way through the entire bunch."

Ollie came up behind them. "Got that stuff loaded like you wanted, Mr. Browning. Now what?"

"Hitch the team to the buckboard. It's going to carry us out of here."

"Wait a minute," Kingman said. "You plan to interrupt the wedding, load everybody on the buckboard, and ride out of here, just like that?"

"We'll try to slow them down," Conrad said.

"Even if we do, they'll catch up to us and kill us before we've gone a mile! We can't outrun Leatherwood in some stupid buckboard!"

"Just be patient," Conrad told him. "You'll see what I've got in mind."

"What I see is that we're all going to be dead soon!"

"And if we are . . . wouldn't you rather die fighting? Wouldn't you rather try to save Selena first?"

Kingman looked at Conrad for a long moment, then jerked his head in a nod. "You're right about that." His hands tightened on the rifle he held. "I've been wrong about you from the start, Browning. I reckon you've earned a little faith."

"Thanks." Conrad hoped that faith wasn't misplaced. "As soon as that buckboard is hitched up and ready to roll, we're going to attend a wedding, whether we've been invited or not."

Chapter 30

Conrad walked over and put a hand on Arturo's shoulder. "Are you all right?" he asked his friend.

Arturo gave him a shaky nod. "Yes, I . . . I just never did anything like that. I've killed men, but not in cold blood."

"That wasn't cold blood," Conrad told him. "Every one of those avenging angels would have killed you without even blinking, if they'd had the chance. You saved our lives and saved your own, too. That's nothing to be ashamed of."

"I suppose not. It's just . . . since I met you, I've done things I never dreamed I'd be capable of. Both good and bad."

"I'm sorry for the bad," Conrad said. "We'll be out of here soon, and then we can get on to San Francisco and finish the job that brought us out here."

"Sometimes I feel like it'll never be over," Arturo mused.

To change the subject, Conrad said, "How did you get away from Leatherwood's men?"

"When I saw them coming, I abandoned the horses and sought concealment in the trees up on the slope. I'm sorry I let them take the horses."

Conrad shook his head. "It was a lot more important that you stay loose so you could help us."

"After that I made my way over the ridge to where I could see what was going on down here. I saw them put you and these other men in the barn. I was afraid they might go ahead and kill you, but when I didn't hear any shots I figured they were keeping you alive for some reason. So I snuck down here and found a rope hanging from a pulley in a window at the back of the barn. I was able to climb it and get into the hayloft that way."

Conrad nodded. That rope was used to raise and lower bales of hay from the loft. There was a matching opening and pulley in the front of the barn.

"That was smart thinking, all the way around."

"Thank you, sir. I've learned to be . . . creative, shall we say . . . when it comes to dealing with villains. Traveling with you has taught me that, among many other things."

Conrad grinned as he thought about the plan he had in mind. "Sometimes being creative is the only real chance you've got."

Ollie came over to them. "The team's hitched

up, and the buckboard is ready to go. But where are we going in it?"

Before Conrad could answer, Kingman hissed at them from the front door of the barn. "Leatherwood's coming, with some of the avenging angels! They're probably coming to take us to the wedding, so Hissop can force me to watch him marrying Selena."

"We're going to the wedding, all right," Conrad said. "Everybody pile onto the buckboard. Ollie, can you handle the reins?"

"Yeah, I reckon," the big man said.

"All right. When we get out of the barn, head straight for Leatherwood and his gunmen. Whip the team into a run and roll right over them if you can."

Ollie nodded. "I gotcha."

The men had armed themselves with the dead guards' weapons. Arturo climbed onto the seat next to Ollie. Conrad, Kingman, and the other two men got in the back.

"Let's go," Conrad said to Ollie.

They had turned the buckboard so it faced the open front doors of the barn. Ollie slapped the reins against the backs of the horses and they started forward, moving at a walk, then going faster as they approached the door. As the buckboard went through the opening, Ollie yelled and slashed at the team, making them lunge into a gallop.

Leatherwood and five other men were only a few yards from the barn. When the running horses emerged and barreled down on them, they tried to scatter and get out of the way, but three of the men didn't make it. With startled screams, they went down under the pounding, steel-shod hooves of the team. Conrad felt the buckboard lurch heavily as the iron-rimmed wheels ran over the trampled men.

Leatherwood was one of the men who had thrown himself clear. Roaring furiously, he rolled and came up on a knee to fire at the buckboard's occupants. Conrad threw a shot back at him but missed as Leatherwood ducked.

On the other side of the buckboard, the remaining gunmen tried to get up but crumpled as bullets ripped through them. That left Leatherwood firing futilely after them as Ollie sent the buckboard racing toward the arbor where the wedding was supposed to take place.

Hissop and the rest of the people gathered for the ceremony would know trouble had broken out, so it wouldn't be possible to take them completely by surprise. Conrad had a hunch they wouldn't be expecting wedding crashers, though.

The sky was gray and yellow with dust. A hard gust of wind suddenly pounded the wagon as Ollie wheeled it in a turn and sent it careening toward the brush arbor. People scattered, fleeing the windstorm. Conrad spotted Selena, dressed in a long white gown, struggling with Hissop.

"Selena!" Dan shouted. "Selena, we're coming for you!"

Avenging angels ran toward the buckboard. Flame spouted from the barrels of their guns. Conrad crouched behind the seat and lifted the rifle to his shoulder. "Keep your head down, Ollie!" he called as he fired over Ollie and Arturo, jacked the Winchester's lever, and fired again. Kingman was beside him, also firing a rifle. Three of the avenging angels spun off their feet as they were hit, causing the rest to scatter momentarily.

The buckboard careened right up the aisle in the brush arbor toward Selena and Hissop. Ollie hauled back hard on the reins to keep from running them over just as Selena finally clenched one hand into a hard fist and drove it into Hissop's face. The punch jolted the elder backward. Seizing the opportunity Selena pulled up her skirt and leaped into the back of the buckboard. Conrad grabbed her while Kingman sent a couple shots racketing toward Hissop. The elder rolled behind some benches, and the shots missed, chewing splinters from the seats.

"Dora! Rachel! Caroline!" a man in the buckboard shouted. "Over here!"

Remnants of the crowd were still scattered around. Three women broke loose from the older men holding them, either their fathers or Hissop's cronies to whom they had been promised as brides. They ran to the buckboard and clambered onto the back of the vehicle as Ollie struggled to get it turned around in the cramped confines of the brush arbor.

"Better get us out of here, Ollie!" Conrad warned. He snapped another rifle shot at an avenging angel and saw the man go over backward as the slug punched into his chest.

"I'm tryin'!" Ollie yelled, lashing at the horses with the reins. They overturned some of the benches that had been set up in the brush arbor as they stampeded back into the open.

Selena clutched at Kingman. "You came for me!" she cried. "You came for me! I didn't think there was a chance!"

"There's always a chance, as long as we're alive!" he told her. "Now get down!"

The women hunkered low as the men surrounded them and kept up a steady fire. Conrad caught a glimpse of Leatherwood and triggered a fast shot at him as the buckboard flashed past, but he was pretty sure he missed.

"Head down the canyon to the salt flats!" Conrad told Ollie. "Fast!"

Ollie looked back over his shoulder. "The salt flats! What—"

"Go, just go!" Conrad told him.

As the buckboard passed the corral, Conrad sent several shots close over the heads of the gathered horses. They were already skittish because of the hard wind, and the shots spooked them even more. They milled around, pressing hard against the poles, and suddenly the corral fence collapsed on one side. The herd broke free, panicking and stampeding. Conrad flashed a grin. That would give them a little more time to put his plan into effect.

Ollie headed across the basin to the mouth of the canyon. A few minutes later it came into sight through the swirling, blowing dust. Conrad looked behind them but couldn't see any pursuit. The air was so full of dust it was difficult to see for more than a hundred yards or so.

The buckboard barreled into the narrow part of the canyon. Everyone held on for dear life as it bounced and jolted. Conrad kept looking back, expecting to see riders appear on their trail. So far, there was no sign of pursuit.

After a few minutes of the wild ride, the buckboard reached the end of the canyon and emerged onto the gentle slope that led down to the salt flats about a mile away. "Keep going!" Conrad told Ollie. "All the way to the flats!"

"But we can't go across there!" Ollie protested. "The horses can't make it!"

"We're taking the buckboard, but not the horses," Conrad said. Ollie looked at him like he was crazy.

Maybe he was, he thought. They would soon find out.

Chapter 31

Ollie brought the buckboard to a skidding halt at the edge of the salt flats, which stretched out ahead seemingly to infinity. The mountains on the far side of the flats where the Valley of the Outcast Saints was located were completely invisible because of the dust storm.

"Ollie, Arturo, unhitch the horses and let 'em go!" Conrad ordered as he hopped down from the vehicle.

"Let them go?" Kingman repeated. "You've lost your mind! You can't mean to walk across the flats. It's certain death, especially in a storm like this!"

"We're not walking. Ollie, once the team is unhitched, lift the tongue and prop it against the front of the buckboard. I'll tie it in place. The rest of you, watch for Leatherwood. If you see anybody coming, let out a yell."

Ollie and Arturo unhitched a couple horses. As they worked on the others, Ollie said, "By golly, I think I know what you've got in mind, Mr. Browning. We're gonna fix us a wind wagon!"

"That's right. We'll nail those boards across the tongue to give us something to fasten that canvas to, and it'll be our sail."

"A wind wagon!" Kingman said. "I've heard about such things, but I didn't know they were real!"

"They're real, all right," Conrad said over the howling gale. And he hoped they worked. He had seen pictures of them in books, but that was all.

He climbed onto the buckboard and tied a rope to the top of the tongue after Ollie lifted it into place. Then he ran the rope to the back of the buckboard and fastened it there as well. They would have no rudder, so they'd have to go wherever the wind took them, but it would be away from Juniper Canyon and that was all that mattered.

The wind caught the canvas when Conrad and Ollie tried to lift it into place, and they almost lost their grip on it. Part of it was free and popping madly before they gathered it back in.

"The rest of you grab the buckboard!" Conrad shouted. "We don't want it taking off on us as soon as the wind fills the sail."

He had sailed on Boston Harbor as a young man, but that was a long time ago. A lifetime ago, in many ways. He realized they should have left the tongue down on the ground and nailed the sail to it there, then raised it, but it was too late for that. He and Ollie kept struggling, and finally they had the sail tied securely in place. The buckboard shuddered as the wind pushed it forward. The men, along with Selena and the other women, held it back.

"All right, everybody on!" Conrad ordered. "Be quick about it! This thing wants to get up and go!"

"Women first!" Kingman said. He boosted Selena into the back of the vehicle as the other women clambered on. Their weight helped, but at the same time the men had to hold the buckboard back by themselves.

"Go!" Conrad told the other men. "Get on there now!"

He set his feet, holding on to one rear wheel while Ollie held the other. Kingman and the others climbed onto the buckboard. Conrad felt the strain on his muscles and knew he and Ollie couldn't hold it much longer.

"You next, Mr. Browning!" Ollie called. "I got it!"

"Together!" Conrad said. "We go together! On three . . . one . . . two . . . *three!*"

Conrad boosted himself up. The wind wagon leaped ahead as the sail billowed. Kingman grabbed Conrad's arm to steady him and finish the job of hauling him in.

"Ollie!" Arturo yelled.

Conrad jerked his head around and saw that Ollie had made a grab for the buckboard but missed. He was running along in its wake as it started out onto the flats, but he wouldn't be able to keep up for more than a few seconds.

A length of rope had been left over when Conrad finished tying the tongue into place. He snatched it and flung it toward Ollie, who made a desperate lunge and got one hand on the rope. "Hang on!" Conrad called to him as Ollie managed to get hold of the rope with his other hand.

He acted a little like an anchor, slowing the wind wagon as he ran behind it. At that moment, riders loomed out of the swirling dust at the edge of the flats and opened fire. Conrad was willing to bet Jackson Leatherwood was one of them. Bullets sang overhead as the pursuers opened fire.

As Ollie struggled to run behind the buckboard, he panted, "I gotta let go! I'm holdin' you back!"

"No, hang on!" Conrad yelled. "Come on, a little closer!"

Ollie was running so fast Conrad hoped his feet weren't staying in contact with the salt crust long enough to cause it to break into sharp pieces. While he hauled on the rope, pulling Ollie closer, Kingman and the other two men returned the avenging angels' fire with their rifles.

Arturo crowded up beside Conrad and took hold of the rope, throwing his strength into the effort. Conrad told Arturo, "Hold on to the rope! I'm going to try to get him!"

Arturo nodded. Conrad slid to the very back of the buckboard and extended his arm toward Ollie. He glanced over his shoulder and saw that

Selena and the other women had joined Arturo on the rope. Between them, they pulled Ollie a little closer, and suddenly Conrad closed his fingers around Ollie's wrist. He locked his hand in an iron grip, and the muscles in his arm and shoulder stood out like bunches of steel cable as he dragged Ollie close enough to grab his other arm.

"Now jump!" Conrad yelled as he hauled back with all his strength.

Ollie drove forward, and Conrad fell backward as Ollie landed halfway in the back of the buckboard. Conrad sought purchase with his boots and pulled some more. Other hands joined in the effort and Ollie slid the rest of the way into the back of the buckboard.

Breathing hard from his efforts, Conrad asked, "Are you . . . are you all right . . . Ollie?"

"Yeah, I . . . reckon," the big man replied. He looked around, a little wild-eyed. "Oh, Lordy! What are we gonna do now?"

"Go where the wind takes us," Conrad said.

The wind wagon was moving breathtakingly fast. The sail was full and straining at the makeshift mast formed by the buckboard's tongue. The ropes holding the tongue and the canvas in place hummed and thrummed like musical instruments from the strain placed on them as the wind wagon veered from side to side at the whim of the gale. Everyone hunkered down and held on.

When Conrad looked back, he couldn't see the

edge of the flats anymore. It was like they sailed over an endless white ocean, only there were no waves.

He felt like he had swallowed and breathed in a bucketful of dirt. The women were coughing and choking, and the men didn't seem to be in much better shape.

"Tear pieces off your shirts and rig bandannas for yourselves and the women," he told them. "We need to keep some of that dust out."

Once they had done that, they seemed to breathe a little easier. Kingman crawled over beside Conrad and said through his makeshift mask, "Do you have any idea what direction we're going?"

"Not really," Conrad replied with a shake of his head. "The wind was blowing away from Juniper Canyon when we left, but it's been shifting around all day."

"So we may end up right back where we started!"

"No, the wind hasn't turned around that much. We're still moving away from the canyon, but I don't know what angle we're taking across the flats. I don't expect to come out right in front of the trail to the pass, though."

"It'll take Leatherwood a couple days to get to the pass, coming around the long way."

Conrad nodded. "That's what I'm counting on. That'll give us time to get ready for them."

"Hissop will send everybody he's got after us this time," Kingman said. "He'll probably come along himself."

"More than likely."

A grin stretched across Kingman's face. "You know, you're a little loco, Browning, but this was a good idea. I'm sorry we got off to such a bad start."

"You mean that business about trying to have Arturo and me killed?" Conrad asked with a wry smile. "Forget it."

"No, I won't. And I won't forget what you've done for us, no matter how long Selena and I live. Of course, that may not be very long."

There was no way to tell how fast the wind wagon was going or how long its route across the salt flats would turn out to be, but Conrad thought they ought to be at least halfway to the other side. The vehicle continued rolling along, covering the ground seemingly as fast as a stage-coach could have.

Suddenly, the buckboard lurched and slowed, then jumped ahead again. "What was that?" Conrad asked as he looked behind them but didn't see any sort of obstacle that would have held them up.

"We hit a soft spot!" Kingman replied. "There are little tanks where water has collected under the crust of dried salt, and when it breaks there's muck under it. The crust cracked back there but the wheel didn't break all the way through."

Conrad hadn't known about that. "Are there a lot of those spots? And how big do they get?"

"They're scattered here and there," Kingman said. "I don't know how many there are, but they can be hundreds of yards across."

That was a new worry. Conrad didn't have long to brood about it. He heard an ominous crackling sound, followed by a sudden jolt as the buckboard's front wheels broke all the way through the crust and sank deep into the salty mud underneath. The sudden stop made the rear of the vehicle fly up into the air. Men yelled and women screamed as they were thrown clear. With a rending crash, the buckboard went on over and landed upside down.

Conrad didn't see or hear the wreck. He had slammed into the ground with such stunning impact darkness swallowed him whole.

Chapter 32

Conrad had the feeling he hadn't been unconscious too long. His mouth was filled with the taste of salt and dirt. He lifted his head, spat out the awful gunk, and looked around.

The overturned wagon lay several yards away. Bodies were scattered around it. None of them were moving, but as Conrad tried to get to his feet, several of the victims of the wreck began to stir.

Conrad spotted Arturo. With the muck dragging at his feet, he reached his friend's side as fast as he could and dropped to his knees. Arturo lay on his back, so he wasn't in danger of drowning in the mud. He moved around a little and groaned. Conrad got an arm around his shoulders and lifted him into a sitting position. "Are you all right? Anything busted?"

"Just every bone in my body, from the feel of it," Arturo replied. He waved a hand. "No, no, I'm fine. See to the others."

Ollie pushed himself upright. "What in the world happened?"

"The buckboard's wheels broke through the crust into a sink hole and it turned over," Conrad explained. "Let's check on everybody."

Within a couple minutes it was clear no one had been badly hurt in the crash. A few bumps and bruises were the extent of the injuries.

Conrad examined the wind wagon and saw that it would never work again. The tongue had snapped, and the canvas had come loose and blown away.

"We're stuck out here," Selena said, panic edging into her voice.

Conrad looked at the overturned buckboard. "We might be able to bust up some of the boards and tie them to our feet—make salt shoes out of them instead of snow shoes. If we spread out the weight like that, we might not break through the crust."

Kingman nodded slowly. "That might work," he admitted. "But which direction would we go? If we start out trying to walk through this storm, we're liable to wind up wandering in circles."

"We're going to have to wait for it to blow over," Conrad said. "That way we can see where we are."

"And that gives Hissop and Leatherwood more time to catch up to us." Kingman sighed. "But you're right. Waiting is the only thing we can do. I just hope it doesn't take too long."

"In the meantime," Conrad suggested, "let's set the buckboard up on its side so it blocks the wind. We might be a little more comfortable behind it."

The men lifted and heaved and wrestled the buckboard into position, then everyone huddled on the leeward side of it. Night was settling down, earlier than usual due to the dust in the air. Shadows gathered quickly, and once the last of the feeble sunlight faded, utter darkness closed in. The dust in the air completely blocked any light from the moon and stars. Conrad couldn't see his hand in front of his face.

Despite the terrible thirst and hunger that plagued them, exhaustion was too powerful to overcome. One by one they dozed off. Conrad felt Arturo's head leaning against his shoulder and heard the soft snores coming from his friend. He tried to stay awake, thinking someone needed to remain on guard, but it was hopeless. His eyes were too heavy, and he succumbed to sleep.

Conrad jerked awake. For a second he thought someone was screaming, and that sent his hand groping for the gun on his hip. Then he realized what he heard were cries of laughter. The sun was beating brightly against his eyelids, and he forced his eyes open, squinting against the glare that came from the salt flats all around them.

Kingman was the one laughing. "Look!" he cried when he saw that Conrad was awake. He flung out a hand to point. "Look over there!"

The edge of the salt flats to the west wasn't more than three hundred yards away. Where it ended, the rocky slopes of the foothills leading up to the mountains began. In the distance, possibly two or three miles north of where they were, lay the pass. Conrad could see it from where he was.

"We almost made it all the way," Kingman babbled as the others came awake. "The wind wagon brought us almost completely across the flats. We can walk that far!"

Conrad pushed himself to his feet and squinted up at the sky, which was a beautiful, crystal clear blue. The storm had blown over completely. It had left some salt heaped up at the edge of the flats, but otherwise there was no sign it had ever taken place.

"Gather up the guns," Conrad told the others. "Hissop and Leatherwood are at least a day behind us, but they have horses and we don't. It'll take us a while to walk to the valley, and then we have to get ready to defend it."

A bleak expression replaced the grin on Kingman's face. "I'm going to blow up the pass. The more I think about it, the more I see that's the only answer."

"But, Dan," Selena said, "that won't stop Father Agony and Leatherwood in the long run. They'll just find some other way to get at us."

"Not if they're in the pass when it blows up," Conrad said.

Kingman shot a sharp glance at him. "You mean lure Hissop and all the avenging angels in there, then drop an avalanche on top of them?"

"That's the only way to stop them for good. Otherwise, Selena's right. They'll find some other way to get into your valley, and they'll keep trying to kill you. Hissop can't back down now, not and hope to have his followers stay with him."

"That's murder," Selena said.

"No, it's self-defense," Kingman insisted. "If they're trying to get to us to kill us, they deserve whatever happens to them. That's just common sense."

Arturo said, "I believe that's correct. People

can't be expected to sit back and do nothing while a bunch of fanatics who want to destroy them plot their demise. Taking action to prevent that is the only sensible course."

"What's going to happen if Hissop and Leatherwood are gone?" Conrad asked. "Will the people who are left behind in Juniper Canyon still try to come after you?"

Kingman shook his head. "I can't guarantee it, but I don't think so. Hissop is the one who holds everything together, forcing people to do what he wants. Leatherwood is his enforcer. Neither of them has ever been all that well liked. People are just afraid of them, that's all. Afraid of crossing a self-proclaimed prophet, sure, but even more afraid of Leatherwood's gun."

"Then you'll have at least a chance to build lives for yourselves in the valley. Some others may even come and join you."

Kingman put his arm around Selena. "A chance is all anybody ever really gets."

Some of the guns had been fouled by the salty mud. The weapons could be cleaned properly once the fugitives got back to the valley. The salt crust broke through several times while they were walking off the flats, but the distance was short enough no real harm was done to anybody's feet.

Once they were off the flats, they set a fast pace, but nobody was used to walking and soon everyone's feet and legs ached. They pushed on anyway, and no one complained too much.

After all, they had come through hell to get away from Father Agony and Juniper Canyon, and the passage to their deliverance was in sight, the pass that waited for them up ahead.

It was the middle of the day before they reached it. Everyone was staggering from pain and weariness as they stumbled through the pass and paused at the top of the trail leading into the green oasis of the Valley of the Outcast Saints. Paradise Valley, Kingman had talked about renaming it, and Conrad thought the name suited it. The place looked as close to a piece of pure paradise as any he had ever seen on earth.

He turned his head and looked over his shoulder, knowing that somewhere out there, riders were thundering inexorably after them, bringing death and destruction.

You couldn't have a paradise without a hell to counterbalance it, Conrad thought. In that remote corner of Utah, those two things were about to come crashing together once again.

Chapter 33

The group hadn't descended very far into the valley when they saw riders galloping toward them. The men readied their guns, but relaxed when Kingman exclaimed, "Those are our friends, the men we left here!"

The riders came up and hauled their mounts to a stop. One of the men dismounted and threw his arms around Kingman, slapping him on the back. "We didn't think we'd ever see you again, Dan! And you've got Selena and the other women!"

"I thought you boys were leaving," Kingman said coolly. "You decided you'd had enough."

"Well . . ." The man shook his head. "We buried the fellas Leatherwood killed and cleaned up the mess from the cabins that burned down, and the more we worked at it, the more ashamed we were of backing down like that. So we decided to stay after all. We were even talking about going back to Juniper Canyon to see if we could help you. But you're here now!"

"You'll still have a chance to pitch in," Conrad said. "Hissop and Leatherwood are somewhere behind us. They'll be here, probably tomorrow morning sometime."

"And we'll be ready for them," Kingman added grimly.

One of the men on horseback asked, "What about Thomas and Todd? I don't see them with you."

"Todd was killed in an ambush at Navajo Wash," Kingman answered, "and Thomas sold us out. He's helping Hissop and Leatherwood now."

The men from the valley looked upset about both pieces of news, but they were pragmatic. "Come on back to the settlement," one said. "You look like you could use some hot food and some clean clothes. How'd you make it through that dust storm?"

Kingman smiled. "You might not believe us if we told you."

By mid-afternoon, everyone had cleaned up, eaten, and rested. The avenging angels had burned down Kingman's cabin along with a couple others, but he and Selena moved into one left empty because its former occupant had been killed in the raid. She didn't like that very much, but he promised to build her a new home of her own as soon as they had dealt with the looming threat of Hissop and Leatherwood.

The entire population of the valley, plus Conrad and Arturo, met there for a council of war.

"Hissop and Leatherwood and the rest of the avenging angels are going to follow us here,"

Kingman said. "I don't think there's any doubt about that."

Murmurs and nods of agreement came from the assembled denizens of the valley.

"Browning and I think the best way to stop them for good is to lure them into the pass, then explode some charges that will cause the walls to collapse on them," Kingman went on. "If everyone agrees, we're going to ride up there and have a look to make sure it's possible. We won't proceed unless everybody thinks it's the right thing to do." Kingman looked around at the others. "I know I've sort of taken over as the leader of this bunch, but I don't want to run roughshod over anybody the way Father Agony always has."

"Dan, if you think that's what we ought to do, it's good enough for me."

The woman called Dora spoke up. "Todd's dead because of those men." Her voice trembled a little in grief. "You can drop a whole mountain on Hissop and Leatherwood as far as I'm concerned."

Kingman nodded. "I figured you'd feel that way, Dora. How about the rest of you?"

He looked around the circle of grim faces. Everyone nodded. There was no hesitation.

"All right, then," Kingman said with a nod of his own. "Browning, you want to come with me?"

"Sure," Conrad said. "We've got enough daylight left to take a look."

The men who had stayed behind in the valley had rounded up the rest of the horses, so there were plenty of mounts available. Conrad and Kingman saddled up a couple and rode toward the pass.

"You know, you and Arturo would have time to slip out of here and get away before Hissop and the others show up," Kingman commented. "We're the ones they really want to wipe out. They wouldn't come after you."

"I'm not so sure about that," Conrad said. "Leatherwood strikes me as the sort of hombre who holds a grudge."

Kingman laughed humorlessly. "Yeah, you could say that. He'd track a man halfway to hell if he wanted to kill him. Still, this isn't your fight. It never has been. But you've pitched in and risked your life a dozen times for us anyway. We never would have made it this long without your help." Kingman paused. "What's in it for you, Browning?"

Conrad shook his head. "Nothing, as far as I know. The only reason we stepped in to help Selena is because I don't like unfair odds. That and the fact that she's a woman."

"A mighty good-looking woman," Kingman said with an edge of suspicion in his voice.

"A mighty good-looking woman," Conrad agreed, "but that doesn't have anything to do with it. You wouldn't have any way of knowing this, Kingman, but . . . I lost my wife not all that long ago. I'm not interested in coming between you and Selena."

"Sorry," Kingman muttered. "I didn't know. I don't know why you were headed to San Francisco, either."

Conrad hesitated, then began telling the story, sketching in the outlines without going into too many details. Kingman listened with interest, and when Conrad was finished, he said, "Good Lord. What a terrible thing, to have your children hidden away from you like that. And to not even know that you *had* children for so long. I'm sorry you've had to go through that, Browning."

"Everybody has their own heaven and hell," Conrad said with a shrug. "I've had my share of both."

They reached the pass, and Conrad took out a pair of field glasses he had brought from the settlement, using them to study the rock walls that loomed on either side of the opening. He saw some cracks and fissures where explosives could be planted and detonated to send giant slabs of rock thundering down into the pass.

"Do you have dynamite or just blasting powder?" he asked as he pointed out the places to Kingman.

"We have a crate of dynamite. That'll make it easier, won't it?"

Conrad nodded. "Yeah, we can direct the charges better with dynamite. There's a problem, though. Somebody's going to have to light the fuses, and it'll have to be timed perfectly so the explosion and avalanche will catch Hissop, Leatherwood, and the other gunmen while they're in the pass."

"You're saying that whoever does that might not have a chance to get clear before the blast?"

"It'll be a near thing," Conrad said.

Kingman nodded. "I'll do it."

"Not a good idea," Conrad replied with a shake of his head. "Selena's counting on you staying alive, and so is everybody else. You said you didn't want to take over this community like Hissop did with Juniper Canyon, but you *are* the leader of these folks, Kingman. There's no getting around that. They need you alive and well, and they're going to need you even more if the valley is closed off from the outside world."

"I can't ask one of my friends to do something I'm not willing to do myself," Kingman argued.

"You won't be. I'll do it."

"Not a chance," Kingman said instantly. "You've still got those youngsters to find. Somewhere out there they are depending on you whether they know it or not." He thought about it and grimaced. "I guess we can ask for a volunteer. Either that or draw lots. That might be more fair."

"We'll go back and talk it over with everyone. That's the best thing to do." Conrad stowed away the field glasses. "Right now we've determined the most important thing."

"What's that?"

Conrad gestured toward the towering stone walls. "If we put the dynamite in the right place and set it off at the right time, we can drop a few thousand tons of rock right on top of Hissop and Leatherwood, burying them for all time."

"I can't think of any two varmints who deserve it more."

Chapter 34

Conrad didn't think it was likely Hissop and Leatherwood would approach the valley until the next day, but since he couldn't rule it out he set up shifts of guards, led by Ollie, who would stand watch at the other end of the pass. Kingman fetched the crate of dynamite and set the volatile stuff down carefully in front of Conrad, who lifted the lid to examine the waxed cylinders. The dynamite looked to be in decent shape. It wasn't sweating liquid hell, the way some dynamite did when it got old and unstable.

"What about fuse and blasting caps?" Conrad asked.

"We have plenty of both. Like I told you, I thought about blasting out some of the springs to try to make them flow better, so I made several trips to the nearest settlement in Nevada to pick up supplies."

"Paying for them with money you stole in those train robberies," Conrad pointed out.

Kingman grimaced. "I don't deny that we've been outlaws and rustlers in the past. Maybe we ought to answer to the law for the things we've done. But that's all behind us now. If we can live peacefully here in the valley, we will. It's good land, and it'll support us." He shrugged. "But if you feel the need to turn us in when this is over . . ."

"I didn't say that. Maybe you'll get that second chance Hissop was talking about. A real second chance this time."

Kingman nodded. "Thanks, Browning. Now, do you think there's enough light left to start rigging those charges?"

"I think we'd better, just in case Hissop shows up sooner than we're expecting him."

They loaded the crate of dynamite in the buggy, which was still in the barn, and hitched four horses to the vehicle.

Arturo said, "I'll drive."

"Are you sure?" Conrad asked. "You'll have a box of dynamite right behind you."

"That hardly seems more dangerous than some of the other things I've done since I've been in your employ, sir," Arturo pointed out.

Conrad grinned. "I suppose that's true enough. Just be careful."

"I'll try not to drive like a . . . how do you put it? Like a bat out of hell."

Kingman slung coils of fuse and a bag full of blasting caps on his saddle, and he and Conrad rode on either side of the buggy as Arturo pointed the vehicle up the main trail to the pass. When they got there, they found Ollie and another man standing guard.

"Any sign of Hissop and Leatherwood?" Kingman asked them.

Ollie shook his head. "Nope, and we been watchin' good, too, Dan." He held up a telescope. "I brought me a spyglass."

Kingman clapped him on the shoulder. "Keep up the good work. We're going to plant that dynamite so it'll be ready for tomorrow."

Conrad dismounted and looked up at the rock walls looming over him. He had brought a pack with him. He loaded sticks of dynamite into it, along with fuses and caps, and slung it on his back. It was a nerve-wracking feeling, carrying that much leashed destruction.

"I can do that," Kingman offered.

"No, I've got it. I've handled explosives before." Just not to any great extent, Conrad added to himself, and not while climbing up a cliff.

"Now it's my turn to tell you to be careful, sir," Arturo said as Conrad got ready to climb.

"I appreciate that. If I get up there and fall, there's one thing you have to remember."

"What's that, sir?"

Conrad smiled. "Try not to be where I land."

"I assure you, I'll be going in the other direction as fast as humanly possible."

Conrad started the ascent. There were three cracks on that side of the pass where he wanted to wedge in bundles of dynamite, and four on the other side. He had to take it slow and careful, so he knew the job was going to require the rest of the day.

It was painstaking, nerve-tightening work. The climb itself wasn't easy, and the knowledge of what he was carrying in the pack on his back made it even worse. He climbed to the highest spot where he wanted to put the dynamite and found a place where he could brace himself with his feet while he worked. He tried not to think about the sixty or seventy feet of empty air underneath him as he slid the pack around and reached into it for the dynamite.

The cylinders tied together in bundles of five would provide a big enough explosion to blow a huge chunk of rock off the wall. He pressed a blasting cap onto the end of one of the sticks. When it detonated, it would set off the other sticks. After attaching the fuse to it, he unrolled some of the powder-laced cord and began climbing down to the second location he had picked out.

When he had the dynamite in place there, he cut a length of fuse from a second coil, attached one end of it to the blasting cap, and twisted the other end securely around the fuse leading up to the first bundle. He continued unrolling fuse as he descended to the third blast site, where he repeated the process. The lowest of the three charges would go off first, but he thought he had the fuses cut properly so the explosions would follow each other very closely, one after the other.

By the time he finished preparing the explosives on the other wall, the light was fading fast, his muscles trembled with weariness, and he was soaked with sweat from the exertion and from the nervous strain of working with dynamite. But he had a length of fuse reaching almost to the ground on both sides of the pass. The stuff would burn fast. If the fuses were lit just as Hissop and the others entered the pass, the blasts ought to occur while they were still between the walls.

Of course, that meant not only would whoever lit the fuses be in danger from the explosions themselves, he would also be smack-dab in the gunsights of the bloodthirsty avenging angels as he did his job and then lit a shuck out of there.

"I've got to admit, I was sweating for you, and I wasn't even up there," Kingman said. "It looked like you did a fine job."

Conrad nodded. "We'll see. We won't know for sure what's going to happen until the dynamite goes off."

"Even if it doesn't completely block the pass,

the falling rock ought to wipe out Hissop's bunch."

Arturo said, "The proof is in the pudding, as the old saying goes. Of course, in this case, I don't believe there'll actually be any pudding. Shall we go?"

Conrad chuckled. "Yeah. Ollie, keep your eyes open."

"Will do, Mr. Browning!"

Conrad, Arturo, and Kingman returned to the settlement where Selena had supper ready for them. Conrad washed up and put on a clean shirt before he sat down to eat. His nerves had settled down, and he felt fairly good, although he was still worried about what Hissop and Leatherwood were planning. Chances were, it would be a straightforward attack, but Conrad couldn't rule out some sort of surprise. Both men were cunning enemies.

After supper, Kingman said, "I think I'll ride back up to the pass and make sure the guards are staying alert."

"I'll come with you," Conrad offered.

Kingman waved that aside. "You've done plenty today. We never would have gotten away from Juniper Canyon if you hadn't come up with the crazy idea of using a wind wagon, and then you handled the job of planting that dynamite. Get some rest, Browning. You've earned it."

Conrad shrugged and nodded. "All right, you've convinced me."

Kingman went to saddle a horse, and Arturo left to go back to the cabin he and Conrad were occupying for the time being. Conrad lingered on the porch of the cabin where Kingman and Selena were staying. It was a warm evening, with just a hint of coolness in the air to make it comfortable.

A soft step behind him made him look over his shoulder. Selena had come out of the cabin. She stepped up to the railing beside him and rested her hands on it.

"I can't believe I'm here," she murmured. "If Father Agony had gotten his way, by now I would have been his wife for more than a day. The first day in hell. It's thanks to you that didn't happen, Conrad."

"And thanks to Arturo and Kingman and all your other friends as well," Conrad pointed out. "I sure didn't do it by myself."

"Maybe not, but none of it would have happened without you." She turned to him and rested her hand on his arm. "And you've done all this for . . . for a stranger."

He smiled. "I'd say it was a pleasure, but that would be exaggerating a mite. Let's just say I'm glad I could help, and leave it at that."

"I can't," Selena said. "I can't leave it at that, Conrad."

He suddenly realized what was about to happen and would have put a stop to it, but she didn't give him a chance. Before he could move, Selena leaned forward, came up a little on her toes—not much, because she was almost as tall as he was —and pressed her lips to his in a kiss.

Chapter 35

"What in the world!"

The startled shout came from somewhere nearby and caused Selena to gasp and jump away from Conrad. Kingman strode to the bottom of the porch steps and stared at them. The light coming from inside the cabin revealed his face was twisted in lines of surprise, confusion, and anger.

"Dan, please," Selena began. "I wasn't—"

"I saw what you were doing," Kingman cut in. "It seems pretty obvious." He swung his gaze toward Conrad. Anger dominated his expression. "And you, Browning, I reckon you lied to my face earlier. I wouldn't have known if I hadn't come back to get some extra ammo before I started out to the pass."

"You're wrong, Kingman," Conrad said flatly. "Nothing happened here except Selena was thanking me for my help. That's all it was."

A disgusted snort came from Kingman. "Thanking you?" he repeated. "Is that what you call it? Looked to me like she was about to *thank* you right into bed! Was that story you told me about being a grieving widower a lie, or do you just not give a damn about your wife's memory?"

Hot rage bubbled up inside Conrad, but he tamped it down and kept his voice calm and steady. "You're not thinking straight. If I was going to make a play for your woman, I wouldn't do it right out here in the open where anybody could see us, like you just did, now would I?"

"You thought I'd already ridden out to the pass," Kingman shot back. "You thought nobody else was around."

"Dan, that's not true," Selena insisted. "You've got the wrong idea. Maybe I was too impulsive, but I was just talking to Mr. Browning, and I felt so grateful to him for everything he's done. I . . . I didn't think, I just . . . I'm sorry. It didn't mean anything. I swear." She glanced at Conrad. "No offense."

"None taken, I promise you."

"Well, this is sweet as all get-out, but I don't believe you," Kingman said bitterly. "Either of you. There's nothing I can do about it now because we need everybody to help us beat Hissop and Leatherwood, but I promise you, Browning, when this is over, you and I will settle this."

"If you're bound and determined to make a fool of yourself, I suppose I can't stop you," Conrad said coldly. He stood and watched as

Kingman turned and stalked off into the darkness.

"What have I done?" Selena murmured in a voice taut with pain. "I never meant for this to happen. I never meant to hurt either of you."

Conrad could have told her if she didn't mean to hurt anybody, she ought to have better control of her emotions and impulses, but he didn't see how that would help anything. "Maybe he'll cool off by morning."

"No. You don't know Dan as well as I do. Once he gets his mind set on something, he won't change it."

"He decided he was wrong to try to kill me and Arturo," Conrad pointed out.

"Yes, but you forced him to change his mind by saving his life, and mine."

"Who knows what tomorrow will bring?" Conrad asked.

While he couldn't answer that question fully, he had a pretty good idea of some of the things the new day would bring with it . . .

Blood, and destruction, and death.

Conrad was up before dawn the next morning. When he left Arturo sleeping in the other bunk and went outside, he didn't see Kingman anywhere, but he didn't look for the man, either. There was no point in going out of his way for a confrontation.

He saddled a horse and rode up to the pass. A man holding a rifle stepped out from behind a boulder to challenge him, then lowered the weapon as he recognized Conrad.

"Oh, it's you, Mr. Browning," the sentry said. He was one of the men who had stayed behind in the valley when Conrad and the others went to Juniper Canyon to rescue Selena and the other women.

"Any sign of Hissop and Leatherwood?" Conrad asked.

"No, it's been mighty quiet all night," the man reported. "I reckon they'll be here before the day's over, though."

Conrad nodded. "I think you're right." He looked at the fuses hanging down the walls of the pass. Everything appeared to be just like he'd left it the day before. The red cylinders of dynamite were hidden in the cracks where he had placed them, and the fuses themselves were almost the same color as the rock walls, so they weren't very noticeable. Of course, once the fuses started burning, the sputtering sparks they gave off would be visible, but Conrad hoped the avenging angels would be charging into the pass in such heat of battle they wouldn't see the fuses until it was too late.

He rode back down to the settlement to get some breakfast and found that Arturo had gotten up while he was gone and started a pot of coffee boiling on the stove in the cabin they were using. The coffee came from their supplies that had been left in the buggy, as did the bacon Arturo was frying to go with flapjacks.

"How does the situation look this morning?" Arturo asked from the stove.

"No sign of Hissop and Leatherwood yet. It's just a matter of time, though. As soon as I've eaten, I'm riding back up to the pass, and I'll stay there until they show up. I'm going to be the one to light those fuses."

"Is young Mr. Kingman aware of that?"

"I don't care what he's aware of," Conrad said. "Some things he thinks he knows, he's got all wrong."

"Ah, yes, the kiss. I'm not absolutely convinced that he *is* wrong about that, although of course it's not really my place to say so."

"Heard about it, did you?"

"I suspect everyone in the community has."

Conrad frowned. "Wait a minute. What did you mean when you said you aren't sure Kingman was wrong about what happened?"

"Well . . . I'm not exactly the most astute observer of human behavior in the world, but I have been around a lot of people in my line of work, and from what I've seen I'm convinced Miss Webster does indeed have romantic feelings for you."

Conrad shook his head. "That's crazy. She's married to Kingman."

"Not officially," Arturo pointed out. "As Mr.

Kingman himself admitted, they simply declared themselves married. There's nothing really binding about it, either legally or religiously. Technically, Miss Webster is still free to be with whomever she chooses, and at the moment she feels a great deal of gratitude to you. I suggest that it has influenced her emotions to the point where she's mistaking that gratitude for something else. Add to that a degree of physical attraction, and you have a very confused young woman who's thinking with her heart, not her head." Arturo held out a cup. "Coffee?"

"Yeah." Maybe Arturo was right, but Conrad didn't like to think so. If Selena actually had fallen for him, it could only complicate things. Once Paradise Valley, if that's what they were going to call the place, was safe from Hissop and his bloodthirsty avenging angels, it would be a good idea for him and Arturo to get out of there as quickly as possible.

If they *could* get out after the pass was blocked, he amended. He was convinced there had to be another way in and out of the valley. There had been no chance to explore it fully. The idea of being stuck there was unacceptable, and not just because of the potential awkwardness with Selena and Kingman.

Frank and Vivian were still out there somewhere. His children, his lost twins, the two youngsters who were depending on him, waiting for him, whether they knew it or not. He would never give up looking for them.

By the time he finished eating and went back outside, more people were moving around. He spotted Kingman saddling a horse and went over to him.

Kingman glanced at Conrad, then deliberately looked away. His face was set in cold, stony lines.

"I've already been up to the pass," Conrad said. "No sign of Hissop and Leatherwood yet."

Kingman grunted as he pulled a saddle cinch tight. "They'll be here."

"I know. I'm headed back up there now. I want to be ready to light those fuses when the time comes."

"I'm lighting the fuses," Kingman snapped.

"We talked about this," Conrad said. "It's too dangerous, and folks here in the valley need you too much. Especially Selena."

He knew it was a mistake as soon as he said it. Kingman turned sharply toward him. "If I get killed, that means you and Selena can be together without having to worry about me. That works out better for both of you."

"No, it doesn't," Conrad said. "I've told you, there's nothing between us, and I'm not staying here. I'm heading for San Francisco as soon as I can."

"Why don't you take her with you?" Kingman sneered. "She'll make a good Gentile slut."

Conrad's hands clenched instinctively into fists. He didn't want Kingman talking about Selena that way, even though he had no real feelings for her except some sympathy and mild affection. Kingman appeared to be on the verge of striking out as well, and the feeling of imminent violence was thick in the air.

There was no way of knowing what might have happened. At that moment, shots rang out up at the pass, their reports rolling across the valley and echoing from the surrounding mountains.

Chapter 36

Conrad and Kingman jerked around at the sound of the shots and stared toward the pass. Then Kingman leaped into the saddle and kicked his horse into a gallop. At that moment, Selena stepped onto the cabin porch. "Dan!" she called as he flashed past.

He didn't slow down. He didn't even glance at her.

Conrad didn't waste any time, either. His mount was still saddled, and he swung up just as Arturo came out of the cabin.

"Grab your rifle and keep it close!" Conrad told his friend. "If they get through the pass, it'll be a fight!"

He sent his horse thundering after Kingman, who had about a hundred yard lead on him.

It wasn't really a race, of course. The enemy forces wouldn't be at the pass yet. The guards had orders to start shooting as soon as Hissop and Leatherwood came in sight. That served two purposes: it alerted everybody in the valley that trouble had arrived, and it would draw Hissop and Leatherwood on, right into the pass where they needed to be for the trap to work.

Conrad's horse was a little faster than Kingman's mount. By the time Kingman reached the pass, Conrad was only about fifty yards behind him. Kingman rode all the way through the pass to the boulders at the other end where the guards were posted. More rifle blasts bounced back and forth between the looming stone walls of the pass, setting up quite a racket.

Conrad was only a couple heartbeats behind Kingman in dismounting. They slapped their horses with their hats, sending the animals galloping back out of the pass to safety. Grabbing their rifles, they joined the guards in the rocks. Conrad dropped into a crouch beside one of the men. "Where are they?"

"Down there about half a mile." The man pointed along the trail on the eastern side of the ridge that meandered down toward the salt flats. Conrad peered around the boulder and spotted about two dozen riders. He saw smoke spurt from rifle muzzles and heard the whipcrack of the shots.

"Their bullets are falling short," the sentry said. "We've got the high ground so we've been able to reach them with a few rounds. I think we may have wounded a couple, but we haven't knocked anybody out of the fight."

"You're doing fine," Conrad told the man. "They don't look like they're slowing down, and we don't want them to."

As a matter of fact, the avenging angels were charging pretty recklessly. Conrad tried to pick out Hissop and Leatherwood, but the distance was too great. All he could see was a group of trigger-happy killers in dusters and broad-brimmed hats.

"Kingman, take these men and get out of here," Conrad said as he lined up a shot. He squeezed it off and saw one of the attackers rock back in the saddle. The man managed to stay mounted, so he could have just been grazed.

"Forget it," Kingman snapped. "You get out, Browning. You're the one she wants, anyway."

"You're crazy!" Conrad argued. "You've got it all wrong, Kingman."

"Uh . . . maybe we should all pull back," the other guard suggested. "Those riders are gonna be here in a couple minutes."

Conrad nodded. "Go! Get back to the cabins and gather everybody outside the other end of the pass. In case any of Leatherwood's men get through you'll have to finish them off."

Both guards nodded grimly, and one of them said, "We can do that."

They took off at a run for their horses. Conrad and Kingman lingered at the mouth of the pass, peppering the attackers with shots and luring them on.

"Blast it, get out!" Kingman said as he levered his Winchester.

"Too late," Conrad grated. The riders were closer, and their bullets were bouncing and whining around the rocks. "You light the fuse on one side, and I'll get the other!"

Kingman hesitated for a second before he jerked his head in a nod. He leaped to his feet. "Let's go!"

Conrad charged back through the pass beside him. Thundering hoofbeats rose behind them. A slug sizzled past Conrad's ear as he veered toward the left-hand wall of the pass. Delving in his pocket he closed his hand around several lucifers he had placed there earlier. He brought the matches out as he reached the dangling fuse.

He snapped one of the lucifers to life with his thumbnail and held it at the end of the fuse as flame spurted. The powder-laced cord caught instantly, giving off a flare of sparks and a puff of smoke. Another bullet ricocheted off the rock wall near Conrad. He glanced toward the eastern end of the pass and saw the riders crowding into it. Muzzle flashes stabbed from their guns.

Conrad whirled away from the fuse and broke into a run again, zigzagging away from the sputtering cord. He hoped the attackers were focused on his running figure and wouldn't notice the sparks from the burning fuse. A glance to his right showed him Kingman had succeeded in lighting his fuse, and was racing for the western end of the pass.

Suddenly, Kingman cried out in pain, grabbed at his thigh, and went down. He rolled over a couple times and came up clutching his thigh. Blood welled between his fingers where a bullet had torn the flesh.

Instead of continuing to run straight for the end of the pass, Conrad angled toward Kingman. As he dashed across the pass he fired the Winchester on the run, throwing slugs toward the charging riders as fast as he could work the repeater's lever.

Kingman waved an arm and yelled, "No, no! Get out of here, Browning!"

Conrad ignored him and stopped shooting so he'd have a free hand. He barely slowed down as he hooked Kingman's arm and dragged the man to his feet. Kingman yelled in pain as Conrad forced him to run on the wounded leg, but he managed to keep moving as bullets flew around them. Conrad's steely fingers clamped around Kingman's arm kept him from collapsing again.

As they reached the mouth of the pass, Conrad glanced back and saw that all of the avenging angels were between the walls, strung out in a line. At that instant, the first charge blew, followed half a second later by the lowest bundle of dynamite on the opposite wall. The terrible roar grew in strength and intensity as the blasts alternated from side to side until all six charges had detonated with cataclysmic results. Huge chunks of rock flew through the air, and even bigger slabs slid and toppled into the pass. Men and horses screamed in sheer terror and tried to get out of the way, but they were too far into the pass to retreat and too far away from the western end to escape that way. With all the sound and fury of the world coming to an end, the pass collapsed on itself, burying the avenging angels for all time.

The wave of force radiating out from the series of explosions picked up Conrad and Kingman and flung them forward, sending them tumbling over the ground. Small rocks and chunks of debris pelted them. Conrad put his arms over his head to protect it as he came to a stop on his belly. Kingman lay a few yards away, trying to cover up in similar fashion.

Conrad couldn't hear anything except a ringing in his ears. Gradually, that died away, and he became aware only pebbles were pattering down around them. He pushed himself to his hands and knees and looked around. A huge cloud of dust that looked like a massive thunderhead boiled out of the pass and climbed into the blue sky. Conrad knew the charges had worked. The men who had been trapped in the pass were all dead, and the pass itself was closed, probably for good.

But his instincts were crying out to him that something was still wrong. As he struggled to his feet, he realized what it was.

"Kingman! Kingman, are you all right?" Conrad's voice sounded strangely muffled to his ears, but he could hear the words, which was encouraging. He stumbled over to the man, dropped to a knee, and shook his shoulder. "Hey!"

Kingman stared up at Conrad dazedly. "What?" he shouted. "I can't hear!"

"Take it easy," Conrad told him. "Your hearing will come back."

While Kingman waited for that to happen, Conrad checked his wounded leg. A bullet had plowed a deep, bloody furrow in the outside of the thigh, but it appeared no bones were broken. The wound needed to be cleaned and bandaged, and he would have to stay off his feet for a while, but Conrad thought he should be all right.

"Browning!" Kingman clutched at Conrad's arm. "Browning, did we get them?"

Conrad nodded. "We got them. But . . . Can you hear me now?"

"Yeah, sort of. Everything sounds strange."

Conrad's ears were getting back to normal. He said, "We got them, but there may still be a problem. I didn't see Hissop or Leatherwood. They may not have been with the others."

Kingman struggled to a sitting position and gave a little shake of his head as if he were trying to clear some cobwebs out of it. "Hissop and Leatherwood weren't with the rest of them? But where could—"

Conrad didn't have to answer that question.

A sudden flurry of gunshots from the direction of the settlement was all the answer either of them needed.

Chapter 37

Conrad lunged to his feet and started toward the cabins, but Kingman exclaimed, "Browning! Don't leave me here! I need to get down there, too."

Conrad hesitated, but only for a second. Grabbing hold of Kingman's arm he lifted the man to his feet. Their horses were nearby, looking a little spooked but not panicking. Kingman's ride would hurt like hell with that bad leg, but it was his choice.

Conrad's brain was racing as he helped him mount up, then swung into the saddle himself.

One: He might need Kingman's gun. Two: He had told the guards to gather the men from the valley at that end of the pass in case any of the avenging angels made it through the avalanche. Three: They weren't here. Four: Something had happened to stop them from coming.

Something . . . or some*one*.

"They found another way in!" Kingman shouted over the pounding hoofbeats of their horses.

Conrad nodded. He had figured it out already. Fearing a trap, Hissop had split his forces, sending some of the avenging angels to their deaths in the pass while he and Leatherwood circled around with the rest of the men and entered the valley by another route. They had taken Ollie and the other defenders by surprise, although that smattering of gunshots testified that some of the men had been able to put up a fight.

However, the gunfire had stopped, leaving an ominous silence hanging over the valley, a silence broken only by the swift rataplan of hoofbeats from the horses being ridden by Conrad and Kingman.

Dust continued to billow out of the pass behind and above them as they raced toward the cabins. Conrad suddenly hauled back on the reins. In the large open area in front of the burned ruins of Kingman's cabin, two figures stood. One was tall and slender, wore a skirt, and had long blond hair that flowed far down her back. The other figure was shorter and stockier and even from that distance gave off an air of ugly menace. Elder Agonistes Hissop had his left arm clenched tightly around Selena's waist, while his right hand held a long-barreled revolver that he prodded into her side.

Kingman had brought his horse to a stop in shock, too. He whispered, "No . . ."

"Come on!" Hissop called to them. "Come closer and see what your sins have wrought! Come and face the judgment and wrath of the Lord!"

"You're not the Lord!" Kingman shouted back in a choked voice. "You're just a man! A twisted, evil little man!"

Selena cried out as Hissop pressed the gun barrel harder into her side. "I'll kill this harlot who dared to defy God's will! I swear I will, unless you do as I say!"

"Play along with him," Conrad said quietly as his gaze darted over the settlement. He didn't see anyone moving around, but he spotted a couple rifle barrels sticking around cabin corners. Hissop's men must have herded all the prisoners into one place, most likely the barn. Scattered around, the followers covered the little fanatic as he threatened Selena.

"If we ride up there he'll kill us," Kingman said.

"If we don't, he's liable to kill Selena. He's crazy enough to do it."

"You don't have to tell me," Kingman muttered. He hitched his horse into a slow walk toward Hissop and Selena. Conrad rode alongside him.

"That's far enough!" Hissop said when they were about twenty feet away. Both men reined in. They were close enough Conrad could see Selena was trembling a little in Hissop's grasp. Her eyes were wide with terror, but there was something else in them as well. After a second, Conrad recognized it as anger. She was filled with outrage that once again Father Agony was trying to control her life.

"How did you get in here?" Kingman demanded. "This is our home!"

Hissop laughed. "You have no home, boy! You are an outcast. You are the banished! God has turned His face away from you, and you are forced to flee from the garden!"

"Juniper Canyon is about as far from the Garden of Eden as any place I can imagine," Kingman shot back. "And you're about as far from God. More like the Devil."

"Don't blaspheme any worse than you already have," Hissop warned. "On the other hand, your soul is already damned to eternal torment in the fiery pit, so what more harm can you do? As for how I and the other servants of the Lord got into this valley of yours . . . you pitiful young fool, do you think you're the only one who's ever been here? I explored every foot of this territory before the angels of the Lord led me to Juniper Canyon! I knew this valley was here long before you did, and I know every way in and out of it. It was child's play to come around from the other direction, enter the valley, and take your men by surprise."

Kingman frowned. "But I don't understand. If you knew this valley was here, why did you settle in Juniper Canyon? The water and the soil and the grass are all better over here. This is paradise!"

"Of course it is!" Hissop cried. "Do you think I wanted a ready-made paradise for my people? How would they ever learn to appreciate what God has given them if they didn't have to struggle for it? I looked at this place and saw nothing but Satan's temptation! I looked at Juniper Canyon and saw how hard work could transform it into a place where my people could live and make their homes without ever taking anything for granted. I saw a place that would be ours because we fought the Indians and the elements and the earth itself for everything that it gave us!"

Oddly enough, Conrad could see Hissop's point. He didn't agree with it, necessarily, but he could understand why the elder had felt that way all those decades ago when he had established his community in Juniper Canyon, rather than in the lush valley on the other side of the salt flats. That wasteland must have represented a stark division to him.

"You're a madman," Kingman said. "What are you going to do now?"

"Why, I'm going to carry out the Lord's will, of course," Hissop declared. "You and all the rest of your sinful followers must be made examples of. You'll be taken back to Juniper Canyon and executed. The two Gentiles we'll kill here. They won't set foot in our home again. As for the women, Sisters Dora, Rachel, and Caroline will be returned to their families and given in marriage to their intended husbands. This one"—Hissop dug the gun in Selena's side again, making her gasp—"has been too defiled to ever be a proper wife for a prophet. I tried to overlook her sins, I really did, but I cannot. She will live among us as one shunned, a servant who will never be spoken to or acknowledged, for the rest of her days. It is a fitting punishment," Hissop added piously.

Kingman looked like he was about to rave some more, but Conrad cut him off by asking, "Where's Leatherwood?" He hadn't seen the leader of the avenging angels, and it was hard for him to believe Leatherwood wouldn't be front and center with Hissop, gloating over the elder's triumph.

A look of sadness came over Hissop's toad-like face. "That valiant warrior in the Lord's service has gone to his reward. Jackson insisted on accompanying his men through the pass, even though we suspected there might be an ambush.

We didn't expect anything as craven as the mass murder you committed here today, though."

Conrad hadn't spotted Leatherwood during those few minutes of bloody chaos in the pass. He hadn't been leading the charge, but his horse could have fallen behind some of the others. If he had been in the middle of the pack, Conrad wouldn't have seen him.

"Jackson Leatherwood's death is one more sin for which the Lord will exact vengeance," Hissop went on. "And the time for that vengeance has come. You men throw your guns aside. We have a long ride back to Juniper Canyon."

Before Conrad and Kingman could even start to follow that order—which they probably wouldn't have, anyway—Selena said in a loud, clear voice, "Don't do it, Dan. Don't give up."

"But Selena . . ." Kingman's voice was twisted from the strain he was under. "He'll kill you. He's loco enough to do it."

Hissop's chin jutted out defiantly. "I am the living embodiment of God's will, that is all!"

"Let him kill me," Selena said. "Better yet, you do it. Or you, Conrad. Draw your guns, kill me, and then kill him. He has to be stopped, even if it costs my life, all of our lives. Kill me, so he dies, too."

Kingman shook his head. "I . . . I can't do it."

A smug smile stretched across Hissop's face. "Of course you cannot. I am under divine protection. The angels watch over me and protect me—"

Suddenly, Selena let out a scream and twisted violently in Hissop's grip. He couldn't hold her. Both her hands wrapped around the gun barrel and wrenched it away from her side. She wrestled the weapon out of his hand and grabbed the butt, slipping her finger through the trigger guard.

Instead of turning the gun on Hissop, she lifted it toward her own head, crying, "Daniel, I love you! Kill him!"

"Selena, no!" Kingman sent his horse plunging forward.

He was too late. The gun roared and flew out of Selena's hands as the impact of the bullet drove her backward off her feet.

Chapter 38

Conrad knew the other gunmen were more dangerous than Hissop, who was disarmed at the moment and not that much of a fighting man to begin with.

But he also knew the avenging angels would hesitate to shoot if the elder was in the line of fire, so he drove his horse forward and left the saddle in a diving tackle, catching the fleeing Hissop around the waist and pushing him to the ground.

Conrad crashed down on top of the smaller man and pulled his gun.

"Hold your fire!" he shouted as he pointed the Colt at Hissop and eared back the hammer. His thumb was all that kept it from falling. Even if the avenging angels riddled him with bullets, the gun in his hand would go off and splatter Hissop's brains all over the ground.

Conrad looked at Kingman and Selena. Kingman had flung himself out of his saddle, fallen to his knees, and gathered up Selena's limp body in his arms. Her head hung back so Conrad could see the bloody streak along her temple. Tears rolled down Kingman's face as he moaned, "No, no, no, please, God, no!"

"Kingman!" Conrad said sharply. "Dan! Listen to me! I think she's just creased. She's still breathing, Kingman!"

Kingman blinked and shook his head as Conrad's urgent words finally got through to him. He looked down at the wound on Selena's head, then lowered his ear to her chest and listened with a tense, hopeful expression on his face. After a moment he let out a whoop and jerked his head up.

"She's alive! I hear her heart beating!"

"Get her out of here," Conrad said in a low, compelling tone. "There's no time to waste. Get her to cover, now."

The avenging angels were holding their fire for

the moment because of the threat to Hissop, but that might not last. He had been stunned when Conrad tackled him, and so far he was just lying there, semiconscious. When his wits came back to him, he might order his men to shoot anyway, even if it meant he wouldn't survive. He was crazy enough to do such a thing.

Staggering because of his wounded leg, Kingman struggled to his feet with Selena cradled in his arms. He stumbled toward some trees about fifty yards away. The cabins would have provided better cover, but there was no way of knowing which ones the avenging angels were lurking behind.

As soon as Kingman reached the trees with Selena, Conrad raised his voice and called, "Listen to me, you men! Come out in the open now and throw down your guns, or I'll kill Hissop!"

From behind one of the cabins, a man called, "You shoot him and you'll be full of lead a second later, mister!"

"I know that," Conrad replied calmly, "but Hissop will still be dead. It's your choice."

Conrad heard muttering from the men but couldn't predict what they might do. At that moment, Hissop tipped the balance by starting to squirm. The elder jerked his head up and yelled, "Kill him! Kill the Gentile!"

Conrad threw himself to the side, knowing the avenging angels would follow Hissop's order.

Guns roared and bullets whipped past him as he desperately rolled for the nearest cover—the ruins of Kingman's cabin. A shot blasted closer and a slug burned along the top of his arm as he surged to his feet. Hissop had scrambled on all fours over to the long-barreled revolver Selena had taken from him and then dropped. He clutched it in both hands and fired as he knelt in the dirt. Conrad felt the wind-rip of the bullet pass his ear as he triggered two swift shots in return.

Still on his knees, Hissop bent over backwards as both bullets drove into his chest. He came up again, like a doll that refuses to be tipped over, but blood welled from his mouth and the gun in his hands sagged. The weapon went off a final time as he pitched forward on his face, the bullet flying harmlessly into the ground.

Conrad caught only a glimpse of Hissop's final seconds of life. As the elder was dying, Conrad was flinging himself behind what was left of the foundation of Kingman's cabin. The smell of ashes and charred wood was sharp and unpleasant. He had hated that smell ever since his house in Carson City had burned down following Rebel's murder.

The avenging angels stopped shooting, shocked to see Hissop's lifeless body. He had believed he was protected from harm by his status as a prophet, and surely some of the avenging angels had believed that, too.

But it wouldn't keep them from trying to exact vengeance, Conrad thought. Taking advantage of the lull he thumbed fresh cartridges into the empty chambers of his gun's cylinder. With a full wheel, he waited for the attack he knew wouldn't be long in coming.

It wasn't. Men darted out from behind cabins, firing as they came, and charged toward the burned-out cabin. Conrad lifted himself enough to return the fire and saw at least a dozen men coming toward him with guns blazing. He could stop a few of them—in fact, he knocked a couple off their feet with his first two shots—but he couldn't prevent them from overrunning his position and killing him.

Kingman pitched in, firing from the trees where he had retreated with Selena, but he was a little too far away to be very effective with a handgun. Once Conrad was taken care of, the avenging angels would go after him and probably kill all the prisoners in a frenzy of revenge. Before the morning was over, Paradise Valley would more likely be Slaughter Valley.

Conrad drew a bead and spilled another man with a well-placed shot, then heard shouts and the whipcrack of a rifle. Glancing toward the barn, his heart leaped as Ollie Barnstabble emerged from the building with a rifle in his hands and fired again. The bullet smashed between the shoulder blades of one of the avenging angels and drove him forward on his face, where he landed in a limp, lifeless sprawl. More men raced out of the barn, firing handguns and rifles.

The prisoners had gotten free! They joined the battle, making the odds a lot more even. Through swirling clouds of dust and gunsmoke, Conrad caught a glimpse of Arturo firing a shotgun, cutting down two of the avenging angels. Leaping to his feet Conrad ran toward the fight. From the corner of his eye, he saw Kingman hobbling into battle as well.

Orange tongues of flame flew from gun barrels. Conrad whirled through the chaos, firing until the hammer of his gun clicked on an empty chamber. As one of the duster-clad avenging angels loomed up in front of him, Conrad crashed his revolver down on the man's head. The big hat absorbed some of the blow, but not enough to keep the man from collapsing, out cold. Conrad picked up the rifle the man dropped and brought it to his shoulder. His first shot with the Winchester drilled a gunman through the head.

He found himself standing with Kingman, Arturo, and Ollie as three men who had managed to get mounted suddenly charged them on horseback. The four of them stood their ground and fired at the same time, the shots ripping out in a concerted volley of lead that scythed through the avenging angels and swept them off their saddles. Three lifeless, shredded bodies thudded to the ground.

And just like that, it was over. An eerie, echoing silence settled over the battleground as tendrils of powdersmoke floated here and there, carried lazily on the breeze.

Conrad looked over at Arturo and Ollie and saw they were both bleeding from minor wounds but appeared to be all right otherwise. A glance the other way told him Kingman was barely staying on his feet. "Ollie, help Dan. Selena's back in those trees. He can show you. She's hurt, but I think she'll be all right. Arturo, you and I had better check on Hissop's men. We don't want any surprises."

Arturo broke open the Greener, took out the empty shells, and slid in two fresh ones. "No, we certainly don't." He closed the shotgun with a sharp *clack*.

"You're turning into a real triggerite." Conrad told him with a weary smile as they made sure all the avenging angels were either dead, unconscious, or too badly wounded to pose a threat.

"I've had an exceptional teacher."

Only three avenging angels were still alive, and one was gut-shot and wouldn't live much longer. Conrad had some of the men from Paradise Valley tie up the other two. "Don't kill them. You're going to need somebody to send back to Juniper Canyon with an offer of a truce."

"Do you really think those people will agree to that?" Arturo asked.

"I think they might. Hissop and Leatherwood were the ones holding everything together over there, and they're both dead. If Kingman offers to leave them alone and everybody lets everybody else live in peace from now on, they might accept it. If they don't . . ." Conrad shrugged. "Nobody will be coming through the pass anymore. Kingman needs to find all the other ways in and out of the valley and make sure they're guarded all the time."

"That sounds like a rather nerve-wracking way to live."

"People on the frontier have been doing things like that for a long time. It's part of the price folks pay for freedom."

They walked to the cabin Kingman and Selena had been using. Ollie was cleaning the wound on Kingman's leg.

"Selena's in bed. She'll probably have a pretty bad headache when she wakes up, and she'll have to take it easy for a few days, but I think she'll be all right. The bullet barely clipped her head."

"She was trying to kill herself, so she'd be out of the way and we could take care of Hissop," Conrad said. "She thought she was about to die. Kingman, what was the last thing she said?"

Kingman grimaced and looked down at his bloody leg. "That she loved me," he admitted.

Actually, the very last thing she'd said was a plea for them to kill Hissop, Conrad thought, but that was close enough. "That's right. I hope you know you don't have anything to worry about where Selena and I are concerned. You can forget any kind of crazy notion about having some sort of showdown with me."

"I already have," Kingman said. "Blast it, you saved my life out there in the pass . . . *again!* I can't very well have a shoot-out with you now."

"You'd lose if you did," Arturo pointed out. "Mr. Browning is quite the triggerite."

"You like that word, don't you?" Conrad asked.

"It has a certain ring to it."

Conrad laughed and turned back to the others. "How did you get loose, Ollie?"

"Well, Elder Hissop left three men watchin' us when he went out with the others to wait for you and Dan. Turned out that wasn't enough. When all the shootin' started, they got distracted, and I was able to jump a couple of 'em and bang their heads together. I guess I banged 'em a little too hard. They're both dead."

"A well-deserved fate," Arturo said. "While Ollie was doing that, the third guard took a shot at him and put that crease in his side, but I and a couple other prisoners were able to overpower him. Somehow in the struggle the man was fatally wounded with his own gun. We took their weapons and came to take part in the altercation."

Conrad nodded. "It's a good thing you did. Another thirty seconds and they would have been shooting me full of holes."

"Oh, I doubt that," Arturo said. "You would have thought of some clever method of turning the situation to your advantage, sir. You always do."

Conrad appreciated the vote of confidence, but he knew Arturo was wrong. He didn't have any sort of divine protection any more than Agonistes Hissop did. One of these days a bullet would find him and end his life, just as his slugs had ended Hissop's. . . .

Unless he gave up the sort of life he had been leading since Rebel's death. Unless he put away his guns for good and went back to being a businessman. A businessman . . . and a father.

But before he could do that, he had to find his children. Pamela had already left a number of traps for him along the way as he searched for the twins. She had hired men to kill him if he came too close to locating them, and Conrad fully expected he would run into more trouble.

The trail was getting short, though. It wasn't all that far to San Francisco. Unless Pamela had doubled back, little Frank and Vivian had to be somewhere between Utah and the Pacific coast. Maybe, even quite possibly, in San Francisco itself. The city by the bay was big enough to hide a lot of things, including two young children. Pamela's twisted brain might have found the idea of hiding them there, right under the noses of Conrad's attorneys and friends, particularly amusing.

"Sir?" Arturo said. "Conrad? You look as if you were a million miles away."

Conrad shook his head. "No, not a million miles."

Just the distance to San Francisco. The last leg of the long, hard, bloody trail.

Chapter 39

"You could stay longer, you know," Selena said with a smile. "You'd be welcome."

Kingman nodded to show he agreed. "That's true. You can stay in Paradise Valley as long as you like, both of you."

A couple days had passed since the explosions closed the pass forever and the bloody battle that followed. The bodies had been buried, and Kingman had sent the two surviving avenging angels back to Juniper Canyon with a letter he had written to Jason Hissop, Father Agony's oldest son and the one who presumably would take over the leadership of the community. In the letter, Kingman had followed Conrad's suggestion and proposed a truce between Juniper Canyon and Paradise Valley.

"We appreciate the offer," Conrad said as they stood on the cabin porch. "Arturo and I need to be heading on down the trail, though."

"I understand," Kingman said. "You have to find your missing children."

Selena leaned her head against his shoulder and rested a hand lightly on her belly. "You won't have to go very far to find your child, Daniel. He's right here."

Kingman's eyes widened as he turned his head to look at her. "You mean . . . ?"

Selena nodded. "That's right."

"Congratulations," Conrad told them with a smile. "I hope the little one is raised in a nice peaceful home."

"He will be," Kingman said. "Or she. Either way, I'm going to do everything in my power to make peace. This valley has known enough war."

"Amen to that," Conrad said. He stepped off the porch and climbed up on a big roan with a white star on its face. He didn't know what had happened to the black gelding, but Ollie, who had a knack for horseflesh, had assured Conrad that the roan was a fine animal.

"And if that black of yours ever turns up,we'll take good care of it," he had promised. "The next time you come back this way, you can pick it up."

Conrad doubted that would ever happen, but he'd thanked Ollie anyway.

A team of good horses was hitched to the buggy. Arturo was on the seat, holding the reins.

Selena stepped down from the porch and leaned into the buggy to plant a kiss on Arturo's cheek. "Good luck to you, and thank you for everything you did for me. For all of us."

Arturo reddened. "I assure you, Miss Webster, I was merely trying to stay alive under difficult circumstances."

"Of course." Selena smiled at him. She turned to Conrad and held a hand up to him. "Conrad, I don't know what to say . . ."

"Then don't say anything," he told her as he gripped her hand.

Kingman had followed her down from the porch. He shook hands with Conrad and Arturo, then put his left arm around Selena's shoulders and raised his right arm in farewell as they turned the roan and the buggy and rode away from the cabin.

Ollie was waiting in front of the community barn. Conrad leaned down to shake hands with the big man. "You're the rock this place is built on, Ollie. I'm counting on you to take care of everybody and help Dan make it a real home for your people."

Ollie's head bobbed up and down. "I sure will, Mr. Browning," he promised. "Good luck. I hope you find your kids."

"So do I, Ollie. So do I."

Conrad and Arturo headed for the far end of the valley. Some exploring had revealed a narrow gash in the mountainside leading up to a stretch of tableland that curved around the peak. That was how Hissop and his men had gotten into the valley a couple days earlier. The opening was wide enough for a couple men on horseback, or for the buggy, but that was all. It would be relatively easy for the inhabitants of the valley to keep it guarded around the clock, if that proved to be necessary.

At the top of the cut, Conrad reined in and turned in the saddle to look back at the beautiful valley behind them. Arturo brought the buggy to a stop and asked, "Do you regret leaving?"

"Not at all," Conrad answered honestly. "This isn't my home and never could be." He smiled. "But I hope it's a good one for them."

With that, they headed west.

Over the next couple days, Conrad and Arturo worked their way back down and out of the mountains and finally came to the Southern Pacific Railroad again. Conrad questioned if they were still in Utah or if they had crossed the border into Nevada. It didn't really matter, he supposed, but he was curious anyway.

He also wondered when they would come to a settlement. They had a few supplies left, but they were going to have to restock their provisions soon. Either that or live off the game he was able to shoot, and considering the mostly barren region didn't have a lot of wildlife, that was a chancy proposition.

Late in the afternoon of the second day, he spotted some buildings along the tracks far ahead of them. "Looks like a little town up there." He pointed them out to Arturo.

"Do you think there might be a hotel?"

"You never can tell. It's possible, since the railroad goes through there." Conrad chuckled. "Are you wanting to sleep in a real bed again, Arturo? It's only been a couple days since we left Paradise Valley."

"Yes, but the mattresses those people use are filled with corn shucks. They're certainly not the most comfortable mattresses I've ever slept on."

"Well, we'll see," Conrad said. "I wouldn't get your hopes up too high if I was you."

"I never do," Arturo said. "That way the only surprises are pleasant ones."

Conrad laughed as they rode on.

When they came closer to the settlement, he saw that it wasn't a very big one. There was an adobe depot building next to the tracks, with a short street stretching north a few blocks. The town had a couple general stores, which meant he and Arturo could pick up some provisions.

There were three saloons, a blacksmith shop, a livery stable, a few other businesses, and maybe a dozen houses, some made out of adobe, the others from weathered, sun-faded lumber. It wasn't a particularly pleasant-looking place, but Conrad was glad to see it.

They went to the livery stable first. A short, stocky Mexican who introduced himself as Ricardo was glad to take care of Conrad's roan and the buggy team. "You must have come far. You have the look of men who are well traveled."

"Too far," Conrad said. "But we have still farther to go."

"Is there a hotel in town?" Arturo asked.

Ricardo nodded. "Sure. The Humboldt House. It's not too fancy, but the bugs won't bite you too bad." He laughed at the stricken look on Arturo's face. "No, señor, I'm joking. There are no bugs."

The look he gave Conrad behind Arturo's back said that *maybe* there were a few bugs.

"Which mercantile is the best?" Conrad asked.

"Trafford won't cheat you. The others . . ." Ricardo wiggled his hand up and down. "You got to watch them a little closer."

Conrad nodded. "We're obliged. Arturo, why don't you go to the store and see about ordering supplies, then get us rooms at the hotel? I'm going over to the train station."

"You're catching the train?" Ricardo asked. "You want to sell this buggy and these horses?"

"No, I just need to talk to the stationmaster," Conrad explained.

He and Arturo split up, Arturo heading for Trafford's General Store while Conrad walked toward the depot. Stepping inside he realized the thick adobe walls kept the building cool. It was a small depot serving a small settlement. He figured one man probably served as station-master, ticket clerk, baggage handler, and telegrapher. Conrad found him behind a narrow window with a wicket in it.

The man was bald except for a fringe of white hair around his ears and the back of his head. In a high-pitched voice, he introduced himself as Percy and tried to sell Conrad a ticket on the train.

Conrad shook his head and said no thanks to the ticket. "Have you been around here long? What's the name of this place, anyway?"

"Why, this is Cavendish. Cavendish, Nevada," Percy said proudly. "And I've been here as long as the depot has. Eleven years, come August."

"You've been in charge of the station that whole time?"

"Yes, sir. Right down to sweeping out the place."

Conrad nodded. "I know this is a long shot, but do you recall a woman who came through on the train about three years ago, traveling with a couple small children and a nanny?"

Percy frowned at him. "Now how in the world would I remember something like—Wait a minute. You don't mean Mrs. Browning, do you?"

Conrad's breath caught in his throat. "Mrs. Browning?" he repeated.

"Sure. The wife of a fella named Conrad Browning. He's a big stockholder in the line, so I went out of my way to make sure Mrs. Browning was comfortable while she and her kids were here. They wouldn't have stopped over at all, except one of the regulator valves on the engine went bad and the company had to send out another one. Had to park the train on the siding for a couple days while we were waiting for it. Didn't want an important lady like Mrs. Browning having to stay in a Pullman compartment when the train wasn't even moving, so the line put her up in the hotel. What a nice lady."

Conrad could have told the man some things that would have proven Pamela wasn't a nice lady at all, but he didn't see any point in it.

"So she did have the children with her?"

"Yep, a little boy and a little girl, as I recall. And that woman traveling with her to help out with the kids. She was nice, too. Really devoted to those young'uns, almost like they were her own."

Conrad was glad to hear the twins were being

well taken care of, anyway. "So when the locomotive was repaired, the train went on west?"

"Yep. San Francisco bound." Percy frowned. "Say, why all the questions, mister? What business is it of yours?"

"I used to be friends with . . . Mr. and Mrs. Browning." Conrad almost choked on the words. It was the first time he'd heard Pamela sometimes pretended to be his wife to get what she wanted. It didn't surprise him. She had always been willing to go to any lengths to get her way.

"Sure you don't need a ticket?"

Conrad was tempted. Surely Pamela hadn't come so far west with the twins then not taken them on to San Francisco with her. He could be there in a day and enlist Turnbuckle and Stafford in the search. He could afford to hire an army of private detectives to scour the city for any sign of the children.

But there was a slim chance that Pamela had hidden them somewhere between where he was —Cavendish, Nevada—and the coast, so Conrad couldn't afford to risk bypassing any of the settlements. He told Percy, "No, that's all right. Thanks anyway."

He went to the Humboldt House and found Arturo waiting for him in the lobby. "I've rented two rooms for us," Arturo reported, "and Mr. Trafford will have our supplies ready for us first thing in the morning."

Conrad nodded. "Good job. I talked to the stationmaster and found out Pamela still had the twins with her when she passed through here."

"He remembered her after all this time?"

"She was pretending to be my wife," Conrad said with a wry smile. "That got her some special treatment."

"I see."

Conrad clapped a hand on Arturo's shoulder. "What say we get some supper? Is there a dining room here in the hotel?"

"No, but the desk clerk recommended a restaurant down the street called Faraday's. He said it was the best food in Cavendish." Arturo shook his head and added quietly, "I'm not sure just how sterling a recommendation that really is."

"Let's find out," Conrad suggested.

Calling Faraday's a restaurant was being generous. It was more of a café, and only a step up from a hash house. But the steaks actually were pretty good, and they came with plenty of potatoes. The coffee Conrad and Arturo drank to wash down the food was slightly bitter but not too bad.

Dusk was settling over Cavendish when they stepped outside. Conrad paused to take a deep breath of the evening air, when a harsh voice bellowed, "Heathens! Murdering heathens!"

Instinct sent Conrad's hand flashing toward his

gun as he twisted toward the sound. He saw a man's shape loom up, saw the sudden bloom of Colt flame in the shadows, heard the roar of the shot. The muzzle flash lit up the man's scarred, hate-filled face.

Jackson Leatherwood wasn't dead after all.

The avenging angel was back.

Chapter 40

Close beside Conrad, Arturo grunted and stumbled back a step. As Leatherwood charged them, firing wildly, Conrad's Colt roared and bucked in his hand. He fired three times. Leatherwood shuddered as each of the slugs smashed into his body. Reeling to the side, he fired again, the bullet kicking up dust at Conrad's feet. Conrad squeezed the trigger again and Leatherwood's head jerked as the slug caught him in the forehead, bored through his brain, and exploded out the back of his skull. He crumpled bonelessly to the ground.

Conrad put the pieces together and figured out what had happened. Leatherwood hadn't joined in the charge of the avenging angels through the pass after all. At the last moment something caused Leatherwood to hold back. He had escaped the avalanche and escaped death, then followed Conrad and Arturo to Cavendish to have his vengeance on them.

Conrad knew it, but didn't care about it. Whirling toward Arturo he saw his friend was sitting on the ground, gasping in pain as he hunched forward.

"Arturo!" Conrad cried as he holstered his Colt. He dropped to his knees and got an arm around Arturo's shoulders to hold him up. "Arturo, how bad is it?"

"I'm afraid I'm . . . wounded rather grievously, sir." A dark worm of blood crawled out of the corner of Arturo's mouth. "You'll . . . find the children. . . . Promise me . . . you'll carry on. . . ."

"Don't worry about that right now. Just hang on." Conrad heard pounding footsteps and looked up to see the hostler from the livery stable running toward them. "Ricardo! Is there a doctor here?"

Ricardo stopped and stared at Leatherwood's body for a second, then turned to Conrad and Arturo. "*Sí*, there is a doctor, but he is an old man and not much good."

"Get him," Conrad grated. "Quick."

"All right. The other man . . ."

"He's dead. He won't ever hurt anybody again."

Ricardo jerked his head in a nod and ran off in search of the doctor. People were coming out of

Faraday's, as well as from the stores and the saloons, drawn by the sound of the shots. They wanted to see what was going on, so they began circling like buzzards.

Conrad felt Arturo shivering as he held on to him. "The doctor's on his way. Don't you die on me, Arturo. Don't you die."

"I will . . . endeavor not to . . . sir." Arturo's voice was weaker. More blood dripped from his mouth as he hugged himself.

Conrad tipped his head back and looked up at the sky, which had darkened from blue to purple to black as the stars came out. Those stars mocked him with their peaceful twinkling, looking down on the scene of death and tragedy as if it meant nothing to them . . . which it didn't, Conrad knew.

But it meant something to him, and once again he whispered, "Don't die."

Percy looked up behind his wicket as Conrad stopped in front of the ticket window. "I heard about what happened to your friend, mister," Percy said. "I'm sorry. How's he doing?"

"He's alive," Conrad said, "but he may not be for long unless I can get him better medical care than what you have here. The doctor says it'll be a risk for him to travel, but getting him to a real hospital is the only chance he has. When's the next westbound?"

"You're in luck," Percy said. "It'll be through in about an hour. You want tickets?"

Luck, Conrad thought as he slapped a bill down on the counter. "Two tickets for Carson City."

Center Point Large Print
600 Brooks Road / PO Box 1
Thorndike ME 04986-0001 USA

(207) 568-3717

US & Canada:
1 800 929-9108
www.centerpointlargeprint.com